the EMPTY CHAIR

An Annie McMuffit mystery

LOIS M. GENTRY

iUniverse, Inc.
New York   Bloomington

The Empty Chair
An Annie McMuffit mystery

iUniverse books may be ordered through booksellers or by contacting:

iUniverse
1663 Liberty Drive
Bloomington, IN 47403
www.iuniverse.com
1-800-Authors (1-800-288-4677)

Because of the dynamic nature of the Internet, any Web addresses or links contained in this book may have changed since publication and may no longer be valid. The views expressed in this work are solely those of the author and do not necessarily reflect the views of the publisher, and the publisher hereby disclaims any responsibility for them.

ISBN: 978-1-4502-4515-9 (sc)
ISBN: 978-1-4502-4516-6 (ebook)

Printed in the United States of America

iUniverse rev. date: 9/9/2010

ACKNOWLEDGMENTS

After devouring countless books over the years by numerous authors, *THE EMPTY CHAIR* took form. I want to thank those authors who have gone before me. I benefited significantly from reading my favorite authors, Sue Grafton, Robert Parker, and Janet Evanovich. I also want to thank friends who encouraged me to write. A special thank you goes to Greta Manville, an author, and my editor and good friend. I deeply appreciate her conscientious participation in making this book as smooth a read as possible. Greta has a unique ability for ferreting out the logical. She shared with me much information about the writing process. My friends, Marjorie White, Janet Jones, and Nancy Norton proofread. Their input was perceptive. I value their hard work. Thank you, ladies.

My gratitude goes to my husband Jerry for his support and understanding during my bumpy, roller coaster ride, while this book developed. He is my Number One fan.

PROLOGUE

MY NAME IS ANNIE MCMUFFIT. I live in the Midwest. I'm forty-five, sixty-two inches measured top to bottom, and I'm not telling you how many inches I am around. Okay, so I'm short with a Rubinesque figure that reveals my weakness for junk food. My ordinary nose sits in its proper place above an often-smiling mouth. I use little to no make-up unless I have one of my few and far between dates, then tend to go over the top with a mixed bag of cosmetics. I've often been told that my curly mop of hair and my eyes are the same color as chocolate fudge. When I hear my married name, McMuffit, I feel like a reject from McDonald's menu. After a painful divorce last year I considered swapping McMuffit for Smith, my maiden name. I kept the McMuffit surname. I believed if I changed it, that would negate the three children my husband and I created.

I now treasure self-rule and have learned the hard way how to fight like a junk-yard dog for what's mine. An unsolicited gift that I inherited from Muley, my father, is a square jaw that levitates instantly at any attempt to bully me. I like to think of myself as a woman with strong convictions but heard it through the grapevine that my grown children often refer to me as, "Granitehead."

Since my divorce and after working ER at our local hospital for twenty years I quite the nursing profession, and ventured into the antique business, a long time desire. Annie's Attic, my new shop, is going under at an alarming rate.

1

MY EYELIDS CLOSED SLOWLY as I shoved the back of my desk chair as flat as it would go. I'd been considering a nap all morning. Sleep would soon be a reality.

A throat cleared. I opened my eyes a tiny slit. A man had entered my office and stood in front of the desk. Beginning at my feet his eyes traveled up the length of my motionless body. When his eyes reached my head, he bent his long frame forward until his tanned face came directly in front of mine. He pushed his face closer and stared.

I heard a long sigh but wasn't sure if it came from him or from me.

My eyelids opened half way. Our gazes locked. He jerked upright and jumped back as he fumbled a wad of papers from his blue work shirt pocket. The papers took flight, flew in the air, then fluttered to the floor where they lay scattered over the green shag carpet. The man squatted, joints popping in protest as he retrieved his papers, piece by piece. He stood up, singled out one and danced it back and forth in front of my eyes.

"Found this ad in the Antiques Appraiser section. Been to two dealers before coming here. They told me 'Not interested.' Hope you can do it," he rumbled.

The paper he waved from side to side was a jagged yellow page ad torn from a phone book.

ANNIE'S ATTIC
ANTIQUES APPRAISALS
Nothing's too big or too small
Don't guess what it's worth
Give Annie a call
Proprietor, Annie McMuffit
1200 West Peoria Road
Peoria, Illinois
319-623-8888

The man just plain appealed to my curiosity and negative bank balance. I set my feet on the floor with a "thunk" from my chair as it lifted me upright. I tried to look experienced enough for a possible money-making job.

"Are you Annie McMuffit?"

"Yes! But please call me Annie." I extended my hand and gave him one of the miniature smiles I hold in reserve for new contacts.

He took the hand I offered, clutching it firmly enough in his callused hand to get my full attention.

"Joseph Carter here. Call me Joe." Shifting his weight from right foot to left, he continued. "Inherited a house from my Aunt Polly. It's jammed with antiques. Everyone down the line in the Carter family had a passion for collecting. They crammed things all over that house from the time it was built. Need everything in there appraised. Aunt Polly's diamond necklace is missing too. I want that found." Then he muttered, "Need to have an auction when the police are done nosing around."

I wondered what the police had to do with anything but put a firm leash on my runaway mouth and never-ending curiosity.

When I was six I would stand in front of the mirror in the bathroom of the house where I grew up, perfecting what I thought was an amazing facial expression. Way back then I imagined "The Look" could convince anyone who saw it that I was a person of mind-boggling trustworthiness with the brains of a genius. I still use that facial expression today when I think a situation requires it.

"The Look" slid over my face.

I've been in the antique business for only ten months and have never been hired for a job appraising more than one item at a time. I could almost hear a Hallelujah choir singing.

Tilting my day calendar so Joe couldn't see its untouched pages, I said, "Today is Wednesday, October 24. Looks like I may be able to work you in this Saturday.

I'll need to examine what you have to give you a fair estimate of time involved, any expenses that might occur, and my fee."

Joe rocked from side to side, right foot, then left, like my children did when they were young and needed to go to the bathroom in a hurry. The chronic mother in me worried that Joe might have to potty. Then I wondered if maybe those moves could be a sign of other anxiety. Joe raked five fingers through his healthy amount of still dark hair that was more pepper than salt. Several random stick-up patches made him look like he'd just rolled out of bed.

He stared at the wall in back of my head for such a long time that I found it a real challenge to resist the almost over-powering urge to turn around and look at the wall, too. When he spoke again I realized he must have been trying to remember his plans for Saturday.

"Let's get it started," he said, "Got a lot to do that day. Might run late. Wait for me. I'll meet you at six p.m. or soon after. Sometimes I stay at a shack next to the Duck Inn in Foggy Bottom. A little burg off Route 24." He gave me the location with vague directions and, with a flip of his hand as goodbye, said "See you then." Joe scurried down the shop's vintage jewelry and clothing aisle and rushed out the door.

Antique buying and selling is almost history in my hometown of Peoria. Poor economy and a major lay-off at our town's bread-and-butter job source, Caterpillar

Tractor Company, haven't helped. The final-notices from my creditors demanding their money had become a daily event. The rent on my shop for September and October are unpaid, and I had no clue where to get the money to keep my business afloat. Maybe Joe was the answer to my urgent need for hard cash.

I walked to the glass door at the front of the shop and stepped into a rectangle of weak fall sunshine sprawling across the floor. I watched Joe make his uneasy way down the street.

He scanned left, then right, then swiveled his head to look over his shoulder. Halfway down the block he pivoted, stepped off the sidewalk and moved to the driver's side of a shiny, new looking, navy blue Cadillac. He slid in. As he sped away I could see JOESTOY vanity plates riding the bumper.

Joe Carter acted as jumpy as popcorn over an open fire. I wondered why.

Going to the stockroom next to my office, I closed its door so no one could see me while I boogied a McMuffit family "Things are looking up," uninhibited legs flying, ass-churning happy dance.

Going up-front again to the refreshment area where I keep hot water, a variety of teabags, and a can of Don Francisco's 100% Columbian coffee. I poured water in the Bunn to brew a fresh pot. Returning to the office, cup in hand, I inhaled the coffee's rich aroma.

On my way back to the office I decided to finish my caffeine intake before rehearsing the interrupted scene of my nap. As I walked past the desk I noticed a small piece of paper cocked up at the edge of its leg. I bent down, picked it up, and could see that it was a newspaper clipping Joe must have overlooked when he picked up the others.

I unfolded it and read:

Carterville police notified Joseph Carter that his aunt, Polly Carter, suffered fatal injuries after a fall at her home. A caregiver discovered Miss Carter's body at 8 a.m Tuesday when she arrived for work. It is unknown at this time when the fall occurred. The deceased, a well-known local resident, lived all of her 90 years in her hometown of Carterville. The funeral will be held at Swinnforth-Morris Mortuary, date and time to be published later. An investigation into her death is in progress.

Hmmmm! It looks like Nephew Joe hasn't squandered his time. Only two days have gone by since his Aunt Polly departed this world.

2

VENUS VENEZUALA IS MY part-time assistant at Annie's Attic. I use her when the income in my business promises to be more than its outgo. I punched in her number. She picked up on the fifth ring. I explained Joe's offer and the huge size of the potential job. I also talked to her regarding the likely solvency this could bring to the business.

"What can I do to help, Annie?"

"Are you available to open the shop this Saturday? And if I'm delayed, can you open the business on the following Monday? Maybe even Tuesday. It all depends on how long it takes to complete my business with Joe."

"I'm available for as long as you need me."

Last month I'd given Venus the keys to my house and shop when I went to an estate auction in the small town of Astoria. She did a wonderful job in the shop but there was a large problem at my house with my cat, Sugar. My neighbor Myrtle called the animal watch society. I appealed to Venus's good nature now and asked if she would look in on my cat while I was gone. I stressed the importance of keeping Sugar's water and food bowls full, and her litter box emptied of contributions.

"No problem!" she assured me.

Venus gives a first impression of being a past-her-prime Soiled Dove. On her job application where it asks for age, she wrote "Downside of sixty." At five foot six she weighs roughly one hundred fifty pounds and likes to wear neon-bright mini skirts that reveal too much knobby knees and blue-veined legs. Considering the fact that I often buy my clothes at the Once Again resale store next to my shop, I don't dress 'by the book' on many occasions. What to wear is a no-brainer for me at work. I wear jeans and T-shirts that my friends have given me with kookie slogans on them. I shouldn't question what kind of outfits Venus chooses to wear but somehow she manages to come across as slightly naughty. Her deep cleavage, small waist, and flat butt are the results of industrial strength push-up bras and girdles.

The fine lines that have crept into her pale skin tallies her years like a tree marks its age by the rings. Her pageboy hair color is anywhere from deep mahogany to a pinky-blonde depending on what week she's into with her dye job. When her hair turns the color of pink grapefruit and the white roots break the surface on her scalp she spends an afternoon in the beauty shop. The next day she has mahogany-colored hair again.

Her generous mouth and slim nose sit under penciled-in eyebrows shaped like fat, upside down U's giving the appearance that she asked a question and is waiting for your answer. A generous application of mascara on her eyelashes makes them look like two big old black spiders crawled up her face and sat on her eyelids.

Venus's soft gray eyes carefully evaluate the world around her. She's as honest as a mirror, helpful, good-hearted, and cheerful. I appreciate those sterling qualities about her.

I'd trust Venus with my life.

On Thursday and Friday before leaving town to meet Joe on Saturday in Foggy Bottom I finished the boring chores I'd put on hold far longer than I cared to think about. Friday night I snuggled with Sugar in bed.

On Saturday morning I showered, dressed, and ate a bowl of honey nut Cheerios drowned in milk while drinking my normal two cups of black caffeine. I spit-polished the house then went to the car about one o'clock and drove to Robbie's Service Station around the corner from where I live. As I gassed up Robbie checked the tires and oil.

He gave a double knock on the back fender. "You're good to go, Annie."

I drove up West Barker; turned right on Moss till I got to Western Avenue then turned left and went over the crest of Western Hill to Adams Street where I hung a right onto Route 24. Traveling south I bypassed the small town of Bartonville where I'd been born.

The trip to Foggy Bottom should have taken fifty minutes. Hours after I left home I arrived at the tiny spot on the map in Fulton County. I did my usual, gawked at the scenery, and got lost. I'd veered right at Little America when I should have traveled straight ahead on Route 24, then ended up in Canton and had to backtrack. I've lived all my life in and around Peoria and Fulton Counties and was familiar with the area but hadn't paid close enough attention to Joe's directions or the map.

Fulton County is located in West Central Illinois and the Illinois River borders its southeastern edge for over thirty miles. Much of the county is farm country and timberland. The many wooded areas and abundant water offer a variety of outdoor activities and really great hunting and fishing.

October is a prime time of the year if you travel in this region. When changing air patterns influence our weather it gives us abnormally warm days in the fall, what we Midwesterners refer to as Indian Summer. The many shades of green on this year's foliage had transformed their colors into a vivid autumn palette of brilliant scarlet, purplish red, burnt orange and glowing yellow. A succession of warm sunny days, cool, crisp, but not freezing nights at this time of the year give the trees a breathtaking beauty in their cyclical display. This year is extra-special because the colors are spectacular. The various types of trees look like colossal flamboyant nosegays that the Jolly Green Giant might pick for his significant other.

Turning left off of Highway 24 at a bullet-riddled sign that pointed the way to Foggy Bottom, population 119, I couldn't remember ever hearing about this place. I crept five miles an hour instead of the posted fifteen down a meandering excuse for a road that finally led to a dead-end in front of the Duck Inn tavern.

I parked my dusty green Taurus among a collection of other cars that looked like they came from a fourth-owner used car dealer. Twiddling my thumbs I tried to relax my impatient, let's speed it up, mind set. Sitting in one spot and spinning my wheels has never been my approach to life. I'm more like the cowpoke in the movies that says, "Head 'em up and move 'em out."

I got out of the car to stretch my legs. That seemed like a good idea until the flying no-see-ums discovered me and started using me for dinner.

A long-in-the-tooth, three-legged, black-and-tan beagle hobbled over and sniffed my legs. The dog looked up at me and woofed a low greeting, wagging its tail in a friendly windshield-wiper cadence.

During one of his rare sober times my ex-husband had bred and sold this type of dog so I had a soft spot in my heart for them. Beagles are squarely built with round, strong feet and ears that are long, wide, and pendant-shaped. They have a black nose with full nostrils for scenting. They're very sociable with a sweet disposition. What I like most about a beagle is their eyes that have a characteristic-pleading look. I've noticed such an expression works to their advantage as they accumulate frequent strokes.

This three-legged dog was about a foot tall and probably weighed twenty pounds. I talked some baby-talk gibberish to him like I often did to Sugar and patted his head. I wondered what the story was about how he lost his leg. The dog soon grew tired of interacting with me and hobbled over to a shack on stilts that sat next to the Duck Inn. Traveling bit by bit up the stairs he flopped down by the door, put his nose between two front paws, then shut his eyes, effectively dismissing me.

Foggy Bottom gave the impression of being a leftover from a grade B movie set that composted for years. Overturned flat-bottom boats that looked forsaken lay at the water's edge of the Illinois River. Fishing nets had been left where they were tossed over low shrubs, weeds, tired looking fences, and from boat to boat. Others lay tangled in heaps on the ground. Clamshells merged with the sandy dirt. Large curved wicked-looking hooks attached to trot lines lay snarled with gallon milk containers some people use for jug fishing.

Discarded beer cans, crumpled into accordion shapes, and broken beer and whiskey bottles lay among tall weeds. Empty plastic grocery bags had fastened themselves onto low bushes and waved desultorily if a breeze disturbed them. Someone's ratty-looking tennis shoe lay abandoned at the foot of the stairs that led to the door of the Duck

Inn tavern. I pictured someone hopping around inside the building while wearing one shoe.

The motionless October air held the combined stench of mud, dead fish, and rotting wood. Most likely the fetid odor was the norm for Foggy Bottomers. I thought the smell was stomach churning.

The river's shoreline thinned here and fattened there as the brownish green water surged to the shore, then with the ebb tide it rolled down river generating a new shoreline daily. Enormous cottonwood trees with their exposed roots twisted and pasty white grew along the river's edge, half in and half out of the water. The roots looked like giant deformed arthritic fingers clutching each other.

Several shacks squatting on wooden stilts huddled near the bar. The Duck Inn's blue neon light reflected feebly from their blackened plank exteriors. The raised houses looked like a covey of hunched monsters lurking in the slithering shadows.

I knew in my heart I would never live in a place like this, held hostage to the whims of weather, water, and insurance company handouts after a flood. Not even the fog drifting in from the river softened the starkness of Foggy Bottom.

It was damned eerie standing out here alone as I watched dusk turn into a black night. I hadn't seen another human being since I arrived. The only sounds I could hear were the river water licking the shore, the far off yapping of a dog, and the repeated chords of a guitar picking out a sad country Western song.

3

THE GREASY SMELL DRIFTING from the bar reminded my stomach that I hadn't eaten since breakfast. It sent several loud, inconvenient "I'm running on empty" rumbles. The closer I got to the tavern the louder the laughter became and the honky-tonk music kicked up in volume. The prospect of food and human contact lured me so I climbed the rickety stairs, pushed open the door, and entered the Duck Inn.

The tavern looked like two singlewide mobile homes joined together, side to side, making one large room. Every curious head at the crowded bar rotated toward me as I entered. I heard one loud comment, "La dee dah, look at the fancy dresser." Then everyone picked up where they'd left off, jawing at each other.

Multi-colored neon beer signs designed to promote sales advertised Pabst Blue Ribbon, Falstaff, and Michelob beer as they winked from the walls. Loud laughter pealed after the delivery of a joke's punch line told by someone at the bar. The place was noisy and a thick blue-gray cloud of second-hand smoke floated below the ceiling. I caught a glimpse of a brass spittoon nestled in wood shavings on the floor, then suspiciously eyed what looked like pockets of snuff tucked in the under-lip pouches of some of the men perched on high stools at the bar.

The front and left walls held a display of black-and-white snapshots, tacked randomly. I assumed they were pictures of Foggy Bottomers. The people in the photographs were smiling widely as they held up award-winning fish and game birds for the camera. This must be the Duck Inn's "Hall of Fame." Also on those walls were six fish, two wood ducks, and a lone goose, each sitting on its own small wooden shelf. Taxidermists must have had a field day stuffing the little cadavers. They were all the identical gray color years of dust settling had produced. They were immobile. Mute! Glass eyes staring at nothing.

On the back wall two doors labeled "Drakes" and "Hens" stood opened on either side of a community sink listing to the right. Just in case someone forgot what gender they happened to be, the Hens' door had a scrap of paper stapled to it with "Female" written in green crayon. Clued in, I knew right off I was a Hen, so took advantage of the 4' x 4' room with its one mucky stool. I exited the room, washed my hands with cold, soap-less water waving them in the air to dry.

My red heels thumped on the wooden floor as I walked to the oak bar that ran the length of the building on the far wall. A large mirror on the back bar reflected the flip side of a hard liquor display.

I asked the bartender for a menu.

"Got none!"

"How do I know what kind of food you have?"

"Jus' ask!"

"Hmmm." A man of few words! Trying for playful, I questioned, "I'm asking, are you telling?" He pointed to a teensy weensy sign propped up on the cash register.

CATFISH TONIGHT

I'd noticed when I came in the place that there was a yard square sign hanging on the outside wall next to the door. It held a menu of sorts but nothing I wanted to eat.

WE GOT UM' HERE
NIGHTCRAWLERS, CRICKETS
RED WORMS
ICE and BEER

I was hungry as hell so ordered the catfish then wandered over and sat down in one of the red fake-leather booths lined up back-to-back along the wall to the right of the bar. I read the top of the cigarette-scarred wooden table to kill time. There were several pairs of names: "Mary Jo loves Lonnie, "Mary Jo loves Jack," "Mary Jo loves Curt," "Mary Jo loves Ed." Each duo of names was surrounded with gouged out hearts. I assumed this Mary Jo was either seriously fickle or had round heels.

The bartender everyone in the place called Jake came toward me. When he got to the end of the bar he coughed up, discharged in the general vicinity of a spittoon, missed, and moved toward me again. After that manly display of non-skill with spit he came closer. Thanks to my lush of an ex-husband, I could tell he was jug-bit by the smell of whiskey that arrived before he did. I could almost see wavy lines, like in the *Charlie Brown* cartoon, representing Pigpen's, disgusting odor.

I doubted if Jake had seen his belt buckle for years unless he looked in a mirror. He was maybe a couple of inches short of six feet with a lardy bottom, and a huge "beer belly" riding out in front of him like a full-term woman. He must be one of those men who has never changed his pants measurement, and brags that he wears the same size as when he was twenty. These braggers keep positioning their pants lower and lower till they ride on their pubic bone—instead of buying a larger size to accommodate an expanding belly.

Colorless, thin lips cut a slash under his offset nose. An earring and his hairless head gleamed with every step he took. The man of few words held up a bottle of Wild Turkey. "Drinks r' included," he said as he poured two fingers of the amber liquid into a glass and smacked it down on the table in front of me like he dared me to drink it. I picked up the glass, raised it in a silent salute, and sent the liquid fire down my throat. It exploded in my empty stomach. I felt like I'd swallowed the sun.

Jake walked to the kitchen area in back of the bar, then came toward me again carrying two white platters overfilled with food. He slid both of them in front of me, grunted in response to my "Thank you" and went back behind the bar.

Two huge, fried catfish rested side by side overlapping the edges of one dinner plate. The second one held a large mound of yellow mustard potato salad, speared by a fork sticking straight up in the air. Red cabbage coleslaw and a slice of seeded rye bread with a roll of yellow butter perched on top, rounding out the meal.

Spreading the butter over the bread with my lone utensil, I got down to the business of eating one of my favorite foods, catfish. I pulled out the fins and broke off the tails of the dark brown, crunchy, cornmeal-coated fish and devoured both while making "I'm in hog heaven" slurpy sounds.

I've often wondered if people who live in river towns have a top-secret recipe for cooking fish to perfection that they won't share with anyone, kind of like a state secret. When you're hungry for catfish nothing else will take its place and this steaming, sweet, white flesh melted in my mouth. It was ohhhh, soooo, goooood.

After I ate every morsel from both plates, leaving only two fish skeletons, Jake came back to my booth carrying the whiskey. He raised one eyebrow and the bottle in a silent question. *Good Lord! The man has quit talking but attempting sign language with his eyebrows.*

I played along with him, mutely nodding my head. I resolved not to down this drink so sipped at it like an experienced lady would. After a short time a tingly feeling trickled down both arms, and everyone and everything in the Duck Inn slipped into blurry slow motion.

Damn! I never could hold my liquor!

It was getting late and I wondered if and when Joe would arrive. I crooked a finger at Jake and when he came over I asked, "Have you seen Joe Carter tonight?"

He managed a curt, "Nope!" and walked away.

I knew that if Joe were anywhere in the building he wouldn't fail to see me because I was one real oddball in this place. I hadn't seen any other women wearing a Cassini black silk suit and red alligator really, really high heels. Millie, my consultant at the used clothing store next to my shop, assured me yesterday that I'd make a lasting first impression if I wore this outfit, and it had set me back fifty dollars. I'd made yet another fashion *faux pas* in my long line of clothing errors. Foggy Bottom was definitely not the fashion capital of the world. I felt as conspicuous here in the Duck Inn as if I stood naked in the center of a stage, blue spotlighted.

The swirling tomato red-and-canary yellow bubbling lights on the jukebox next to the front door tempted me, so I wandered over and fed its hungry little stainless steel mouth. I placed a quarter in the round slot, pushed in its shiny tongue, and punched B2. Whirr! Whirr! Clank! Clunk! Inside the glass cage a mechanical arm pivoted with a round black disc clutched in its motorized claw-like hand. The claw then gently placed a recording into a pre-ordained slot.

Well dang it! I wanted to hear "On the Road Again," a Willie Nelson favorite of mine, but Patsy Cline was belting out her years' old hit song "Crazy." After that song fiasco someone else fed the jukebox and a different song began with a lot of "Achey Breaky" heart words. As if on cue, seven women in the bar hustled to the middle of the floor and started a line dance. Dirty tennis shoes and ass-hugging blue jeans seemed to be the female dress code for the Duck Inn.

"This ones on me," Joe said as he reached over and topped off the whiskey in my glass.

4

"PAST THE TEETH, OVER THE GUMS," look out stomach here it comes," Joe recited in a singsong drawl. I thought that little ditty might be considered poetry here in this neck of the woods. He downed his glass of whiskey like it was water as his prominent Adam's apple bobbed up and down.

Joe had arrived at seven-thirty, one-and-one-half-hours late. I'd arrived early, and after waiting for him since five o'clock I wasn't the best me that I could be. My mental powers had diminished substantially after every drink. Desperately trying to make my tongue behave, I said, "Joe, I need shome shleep. My brain's ashleep, but not the rest of me. Nothin' works right. Le's have a meetning tomorror?'

He laughed as if I'd told him a joke, then said, "OK, Annie."

"Any clean motels aroun' here, Joe?"

"Are you okay to drive?"

"I'm a good driver."

"The house we'll be looking through tomorrow is in Carterville. Fifteen miles farther down the highway. There's a motel right there on Route 24. The Sleep Inn. On the edge of town as you go in. Meet you out in front of it at eight in the morning." He stood up to leave. "Have them put your room charge on my tab. Have some black coffee before you leave. Promise?"

"Okey, Dokey!" *How unusual, I've never known anyone who ran a tab at a motel.*

After Joe left, the Saturday night crowd slowly increased. The volume of the music, the amount of Wild Turkey I'd drunk, and the thumping feet on the wooden floor made me feel like I was sitting inside a drum. One local at the bar kept raising and lowering his black wooly-worm eyebrows up and down at my eye contact. What is it with this silent facial language in the boondocks? When he started that eyebrow wriggling business my first thought was that he must have something in his eyes bothering him. Then he started making kissy moves with his big old fat wet lips while watching me with a goofy look on his face. I wondered if the man was a few sandwiches short of a picnic. But then again, maybe that little routine was his method of flirting. *Yikes!*

Jake, the bartender, slid into my booth on the opposite seat with his nearly empty bottle of Wild Turkey raised. "Last call?"

He was close enough to me that I got the full blast of his 100-proof breath. His red-rimmed, piggy eyes found a home in my cleavage. I hadn't liked the creepy feeling I'd been getting this past hour when I caught Jake's eyes on me. I shook my head no, slid out of the booth, paid my bill and zigzagged out the door making a less than lady-like exit from the tavern. On the landing, I grabbed the railing to steady my clumsy progress down the stairs.

When I got to my car I slid in, locked the doors, fastened my seatbelt, and backtracked to Route 24. Keeping the car on my side of the road's white line was a major accomplishment. I made my muzzy way to Carterville. The Sleep Inn motel came at me out of the dark from nowhere as I rounded a curve. I parked next to the office and noticed there were six units lined up facing Route 24. Each stood about a foot from the other. They looked as if they were propping each other up. The front of each unit had been painted a different vibrant color. I couldn't see any cars parked in front of the units that would indicate somebody was staying here, but it was early. The by-the-hour crowd probably hadn't arrived yet. But the motel looked clean. My only option was to drive back to Peoria. No thank you! I decided to stay.

I entered the office and checked in.

The young male clerk explained, "This motel don't go by room numbers. Each unit is assigned a different color. Since you're alone I'll give you the room closest to the office here," and handed me the key to the "Blue Room."

That key was attached to a ping-pong paddle, painted a brilliant shade of sapphire-colored enamel. The damned thing was so big and awkward it wouldn't even fit in my purse. I looked at the empty space where my paddle had been hanging alongside five others and could tell that the banana yellow, grass green, eggplant purple, lipstick red, and burnt orange rooms hadn't been rented tonight. I'd bet a dollar to a twenty this motel had never had a customer drive off with one of their keys.

The temperature must have dropped thirty degrees after the sun went down. I was so cold my teeth were clickety-clacking. I hurried out to my car and drove to the blue room. I grabbed my overnight case from the trunk. Fumbling around in the dark, I slipped the key into the keyhole, then felt, and smelled someone's hot breath stirring the short hairs on the back of my neck. Wheeling around, I found Jake nearly glued to my back. My whole body puckered up.

"Damn it!" I yelled. "Get the hell away from me, Jake, or I'll scream so loud the police in Peoria County will hear me."

I dropped my case, wheeled around, and shoved him hard. Caught off guard he stumbled backward, staggering as he tried to catch his balance. I sidestepped into the room and slammed the door in his face. I rammed the lock in place and hooked the chain.

"You snooty bitch, you've been comin' on to me all night," boomed into my room.

I was terrified, but noticed that the man of few words could string a whole sentence together when he wanted to. Pulling the drape away from the window I peeked out and saw Jake weaving away from my door towards a red pickup. He climbed in his truck and wheeled it in a U-turn out onto the highway, spitting gravel and laying rubber back in the direction of Foggy Bottom.

I tried to puzzle out what I should do next, but my thoughts were too disordered to make sense of them. I was exhausted and had gone way beyond my drinking capacity.

Should I stay? Should I go? The lure of money-money-money seduced me.

Cranking up the thermostat I kicked off my shoes and struggled out of my suit. I zipped open the travel case that I've hauled around in the trunk of the car since my divorce. I often let my imagination run rowdy. Topping the list of possibilities that I fantasize about is my getting lucky and having a handsome prince of a man, definitely not a Jake, plead with me to stay the night. It's never happened, but it doesn't cost a thing to let my thoughts follow a path filled with endless possibilities.

I lined up my toothbrush, toothpaste, jeans, underwear, T-shirt, and Reeboks on the top of the bureau at the foot of the bed. I put on the mega-sized Mickey Mouse T-shirt that I sleep in.

Sitting down on the side of the bed I bounced a few times to check its softness. That didn't help the pounding headache I'd been nurturing. I fell over sideways with a whimper and pulled the thin bedspread over my tired self. My brain turned off.

5

THE COVERS FLEW IN THE AIR as I shot out of bed. My bare feet landed in the middle of a gritty used up carpet. Adrenaline pumped! Heart raced! A nerve-shattering racket ricocheted around the room, bouncing off the walls, and rattling the windowpane. My imagination kicked in and I pictured a wild maniac running amok with a chain saw. I eased the drape back an inch and peeked out the window expecting to see a chain saw killer slaughtering people.

A lone workman aggressively trimming a tree came into view.

I lay back down and patted my chest while trying to get my heart rate back to normal. Then I tried to figure out where in the hell I was and why wasn't I in my own pink frilly bedroom. I looked around the 12-foot x 12-foot room that had more than a few shades of blue. Sapphire paint covered the walls and ceiling. The drapes were a dusty cotton print with faded blue cabbage roses on them. The rug was a stained cornflower color. The threadbare aqua-and-lime striped bedspread needed laundering, or maybe the trash-bin. A two-foot square poster of tropical fish hung on the wall above the bed's headboard in a vain attempt at good taste. A large gray cobweb drooped in the corner of the ceiling by the bathroom door. I obsessed for a while about the possible gigantic size of the spider that produced it. The "easy" chair by the window was a slatted wooden fold-up affair.

The room smelled like old dust, old cigarette smoke, and old sex.

With every beat of my heart my head throbbed in a synchronized rhythm. My mouth tasted like a month-old newspaper on the bottom of a well-used birdcage. I went into the bathroom, downed three aspirin, and brushed my teeth.

Then I remembered last night and the trouble I'd had with Jake. Someone needed to teach him the difference between a woman coming on to him and plain, old-fashioned good manners. It sure as hell wouldn't be me. I decided to never go back to the Duck Inn. If Jake pestered me again I'd turn him in to the local police.

The outsized pain in my head had started to ease. After a shower I dried off with a gray towel I could have read the *Daily Times* through. I dressed in fresh underwear, blue jeans, white T-shirt, and Reeboks, my work clothes. Most of my T-shirts have witty bumper sticker sayings on them. For the meeting today with Joe I picked out the least obnoxious one I had with me. It read, "There are three kinds of people, those who can count, and those who can't."

Our weather in Illinois can drop dramatically at this time of the year, going from sixty degrees to thirty in an hour. I always keep a warm, down-filled jacket and a lightweight wool sweater in the car in case of weather changes. Grabbing the jacket out of the car I threw it over my shoulders. Tucking the blue ping-pong key paddle under my arm I trotted around the building to the back of the office where the local Donut Shop was attached like an afterthought to the building.

The donut and coffee aroma wafted in the air. My brain identified a below-normal caffeine level. My body's stalled early morning engine revved up with the promise of coffee. Pushing open the door I could see all three booths in the place were full so I perched on one of the three counter stools. In front of me was a sign that read,

STOOLS FOR TEN MINUTE
IN AND OUT
CUSTOMERS ONLY

Monica's nametag rode majestically over her two enormous boobs. She could have balanced dinner plates on them as she swished over and stood in front of me. She swiped at the counter with the corner of her apron completely missing the crumbs in front of me.

"Watcha' want?" Pop went her gum.

"Black coffee and a chocolate-covered donut."

"That it?"

I borrowed Jake, the bartender's man of few words style and said, "Yep."

Monica slid a Styrofoam cup of coffee and a paper-wrapped donut toward me. She snagged the five-dollar bill that I'd laid on the counter. As she put my change in front of me, she offered up, "Ya' got six minutes more to sit on that stool. Then ya' haf'ta move to a booth or leave." Pop, pop went the gum.

There were only three stools and three booths in this dinky hole in the wall. They held a noisy crowd. My morning fantasy of slowly sipping black coffee and nibbling my way around the chocolate icing on a donut would have to be a breakfast picnic in the car. I left and went back around the building to the Blue Room to sit in my car.

Joe told me last night that he'd meet me at eight this morning. It was seven forty-five. I finished my coffee and donut, then licked the chocolate stuck to the paper wrapping while I watched for Joe. Last night I judged him to be pushing sixty. The scent he wore was something with sandalwood in it. I recognized it because I associate that particular smell with my insufferable ex-husband, whom I haven't seen since the judge ordered him to pay $1,000 a month in alimony.

I saw Joe coming toward me, followed by the three-legged dog from Foggy Bottom. I got out of my car and stood next to it as he approached. His hand was outstretched and a smile turned up the corners of his mouth but didn't quite make it to his eyes.

"Hello again, Annie."

His low voice sounded gravelly this morning. He wore black jeans paired with a white dress shirt on his long-limbed body. A tweed jacket with those cute little leather patches on the elbow areas completed the ensemble. I've often wondered if those patches were sewn on men's jackets to cover a hole, or if they were there only for decoration.

Joe wore white really, really big sneakers and I knew he'd never be able to sneak up on anyone with his more-than-generous feet. He seemed youthful for his apparent age. His graying hair, more dark than white had been styled in a holdover from his youth, a "duck's ass," DA for short. A deep dimple in his chin and eyes the color of stone-washed denim in his angular face made him look like an older version of John Travolta. He oozed a generous amount of masculinity. I thought that he must have been a heartbreaker in his young days and wondered if he could make the moves Travolta did on the dance floor when he'd starred in *Grease*, and *Saturday Night Fever*.

Looking down at the three-legged beagle I'd seen in Foggy Bottom last night, I asked, "Who's your friend?"

Joe bent and jiggled the dog's ears from side to side. "Name's Sparky. Been my pal fourteen years."

"How'd Sparky lose the leg?"

"Oh, Dad and I used dynamite to grub stumps on our farm years ago. Sparky chased a rabbit too close. When the load exploded Sparky and the rabbit wheeled in the air. When they landed my dog was minus a leg. The rabbit was a fur ball."

Sparky snuffled all over my feet, wetting my shoes with slobbers. I rewarded him with a pat on the head and a "Good boy," for smearing my Reeboks with dog spit.

"Follow me, Annie. You'll see what real chaos looks like."

I tried to memorize the route Joe was taking so I'd be able to find my way back to the motel later.

Like all rural towns that I've been to, the people who live there don't or won't provide directions using actual street names. They seem to go by landmarks, some of which may no longer exist. I asked the young clerk at the motel last night where I could find the old Carter house. He gave me the expected small town directions.

"Go past the bank and the old Smith place, turn right where the Donut Hole used to be before it moved here, then go past the Carter Hospital and you'll see a little white house with green shutters. Amy's old place." He sucked in more air, then continued, "Turn left there and keep going till you come to a big old scary place sitting on one city block. That will be the old Carter house."

I was happy to have Joe lead the way today. He pulled up to a curb and parked his car in front of a red brick, weathered to soft pink, Victorian house and stood in front

33

of it waiting for me. I parked behind his car, slid out, walked over to Joe.

We both stared up at a mind-blowing three-story house. A twelve-foot high, black wrought iron fence encircled the grounds, and the house that sat in the middle of one city block. A long curved gravel drive led to two massive double doors at the front entrance.

The Carter home must have been built in the late 1800s when this type of house was common. A wraparound porch enclosed the front and north side of the house. Latticework decorated the railings and its round columns propped up an unstable-looking roof that sheltered the porch from the elements. On the south side a porte-cochere, built to accommodate carriages, remained intact. The house flaunted multiple rooflines that had an assortment of pitches. Gingerbread detailing hugged the roof edges. A round turret caught my eye.

A widow's walk on the highest pointed roof, called a witch's cap, was located in the center of the roof and about three feet wide. It encircled a brick chimney. I could see the middle part of the wooden railing on the south side was missing a section. A small piece of something yellow flapped from it in the wind.

Dense untidy bushes and weeds had taken over the excuse of a yard surrounding the house. Unruly dark green ivy crawled over the structure, its leaves beginning to brown and curl as they slowly surrendered to the colder weather. The ivy threatened to cover the many tall windows that stared back at us. A crowded stand of tall oak trees towered eighty to a hundred feet in the air. Their dying leaves created a canopy that effectively blocked sunrays from penetrating to the bare ground beneath. On the south side of the property I could see a garage with what appeared to be living quarters above, judging from the lace curtains and flowerpots in the windows. Several outbuildings must have been in recent use because the surrounding space looked tidy. Lichen-covered stone foundations and rotted wood was all that was left behind where other out buildings had once stood.

The tract houses scattered on postage stamp lots near the Carter house seemed pocket-sized in contrast to this building's large scale. Joe's newly acquired house appeared out of place, and out of time.

Joe filled me in about the origins of the house. "It was built in 1868 by Carl Carter, my great, great grandfather. He was a master carpenter. Relocated to this region from Sedalia, Missouri. Only Carter families have lived in it ever since. The house has been renovated several times over the years. Used to be fifteen rooms. With all the changes there are only ten now." He stopped to pull a thriving weed from the middle of the walkway. "During the time of slavery it was used as a branch of the Underground Railroad.

"Let's do a walk-through, Annie. You'll see all the upstairs rooms are crammed full of junk. In the muddle you'll find trash among treasures. There are collections of furniture, jewelry, silver, china, crystal and knick-knacks. Some of the things date to when the house was built and even before. Like I said, Aunt Polly was a saver. Matter of fact everyone in the Carter family could be called a collector. Must be some quirk in their nature that started way back when."

Joe squatted, jerked an enormous dandelion up by its roots, and tossed it away from the path.

"I'm the last one alive in the Carter family. That fixated foolishness ends with me."

6

SITTING PATIENTLY ON THE GROUND at Joe's feet, Sparky was gazing up into his face. As soon as Joe pushed open the gate the dog took off like a missile, barking as he ran around in circles with his nose to the ground. He disappeared from view among the oak trees in back of the house. Joe and I crunched our way up the curved, weedy, gravel drive and climbed gingerly up six decaying wooden stairs.

Taking a large ornate iron key from his pants pocket, Joe unlocked the tall double doors. He opened them to the accompanying sounds of a haunted house squeal. With my undisciplined imagination I had a feeling that there might be any number of things inside that could go thunkity, tap, or clatter in the night.

Ushering me into the musty-smelling house, Joe gave a rolling wave of his hand, saying, "Trying to organize things. This is as far as I got. Shoveled stuff in these boxes from the rooms downstairs. Upstairs is still a littered mess. Tried to have the house cleaned out several times when Aunt Polly was alive. It always sent her into a frenzy, so I'd admit defeat."

The twelve-foot high ceiling in the entry hall and the winding oak staircase located to our right echoed our slow progress. Cardboard boxes advertising Oxydol laundry detergent, Van Camp's pork and beans, Libby's sauerkraut, Charmin, and an assortment of other edibles and paper goods were stacked along both walls. Joe must have raided every grocery store alley Dumpster he could find. Box on top of box had been stacked way above my eye level.

A dirty stained-glass transom over the top of the double doors depicted a quiet pastoral scene. The early morning sun shining through the glass set off a display of white, red, yellow and blue diamond-like sparkles that danced over the floor, walls, ceiling, and the piled up boxes.

I felt like I was standing inside a rainbow. *Awesome!*

Joe disappeared into a spacious room on the south side of the entry hall, so I scuttled after him.

"This large room was created years ago by combining two parlors, Annie."

As though pulled by an unseen cord, I walked to the white marble fireplace on the far side of the room and stared up at a life-sized portrait above the mantle. A beautiful young woman with the slightest of smiles gazed serenely down at me.

"Aunt Polly in her glory days," Joe said in my ear. I'd been so captivated by the image that I hadn't heard him approach so close.

In the painting his Aunt Polly's flaxen hair, pulled back in a chignon, sat low on the back of her head, a style popular many years ago. Porcelain-like skin, stretched taut over the oval face, emphasized the high cheekbones. Silvery, wing-like brows flew above her cobalt eyes, giving the impression that she looked directly into mine. Her parted pink rosebud lips, under a small nose, seemed ready to speak. Her dress was an off-the-shoulder, floor-length gown pooling at her feet, its color matching her eyes. Around that delicate neck a triple-strand diamond necklace rested low on her chest with one large oval-shaped stone partially hidden under a pleat of the bodice. The necklace looked like a museum piece.

Joe pointed to the painting. "See that necklace? Aunt Polly got it from her one and only admirer on her twentieth birthday. Necklace is probably worth a small fortune now. Never had it appraised. If I asked her about it, she'd say, 'that'd be plain foolishness. It's worth to me has no price tag.'"

"Where is it now, Joe?"

"Don't know. Can't find it. She never ate a meal unless the damned thing was strung around her neck. Raised a ruckus if it wasn't. I looked through everything in those boxes out in the hall. Didn't find it. Keep your eyes peeled!"

A crystal chandelier in the center of the room tinkled as though some unseen hand had set it in motion. When the sun's rays from the tall, narrow east windows in the front of the room touched it, the chandelier glittered like Polly's diamond necklace must have when displayed around her neck.

We did a walk-through in the downstairs rooms. I could tell the glowing oak woodwork was in its original state, not painted, as many of the older homes had been when updated by occupants. There were four fireplaces in the main downstairs rooms. Wavy, bubbly, original glass remained intact in the windows.

We came to a library with ceiling-high shelves crammed full of dusty, musty-smelling books. I wanted to examine each and every one if I took this job. Always the optimist, I thought maybe I would discover a few first editions or perhaps one with the center cut out to conceal valuables.

From the library we entered directly into a formal dining room. A massive mahogany table sat in the center and a wide matching sideboard was positioned along the far wall. Eighteen tall-backed, brocade upholstered chairs graced the sides and ends of the table, awaiting dinner guests to occupy them. The table was covered with a lace cloth and set with dinnerware in a Queen Anne pattern. *Beautiful!*

A butler's pantry was directly off a modernized kitchen, its numerous cupboards reaching the ceiling. The shelves held several sets of elegant dinner service and one large collection of Flow Blue fine china. Lined drawers were filled with surprisingly tarnished silver. Another cupboard held cooking implements. Pocket doors had been employed in the downstairs rooms to accommodate a large gathering of guests. The two rooms could be easily transformed into one large entertainment area by shoving the sliding doors into the opening between the walls.

As Joe and I went up the winding staircase off the front hall, I examined the fantastic candlestick oak spindles, still in excellent condition. The second floor was cluttered but easily negotiated. The third floor rooms were chaotic, just as Joe had described. A skinny path to get from one room to another wound through a mixture of hoarded possessions in the hallway, barely wide enough for one person to pass through. Joe maneuvered the shoulder high mess by turning sideways and raising his arms over his head at different points along what could only be called a trail. I'm built narrower and much shorter than Joe, so found my way through without a problem, but the clutter above my head made me feel claustrophobic.

The information I'd gleaned, seen, and heard about Polly sounded like the typical symptoms of a disordered mind. I felt a great sadness for the beautiful woman who'd lived here in that shadowed world.

Joe and I spent a good portion of the morning poking through the house while we considered what needed to be done and where to start. We still hadn't looked through the attic. After what I'd seen—and if I took this job—I would probably start organizing my work up there, then move things down and out after the inventory.

The house was warm. I'd shed my jacket earlier, so put it back on as we stepped out the kitchen door and down the six steps ending at ground level.

Joe gave an ear-piercing whistle. Immediately, Sparky ran to us from under the trees and dropped something at Joe's feet. Joe squatted to pat the dog's head, rewarding him with a "Good boy." He picked up Sparky's offering, stood and palmed it, then held it out in front of me so I could see what it was. It looked like a small piece of faded cloth. "When we come here Sparky brings me presents like this. Don't know where he finds these things."

Joe stepped away and pointed to a large building that looked like a carriage house converted to a three-car garage with living quarters overhead. "I stay up there now and again when I come to town. It's comfortable. Phone works. Water and electric's on. There's a bedroom, and an all-purpose living section. There's a desk and galley kitchen too. If this job takes as long to complete as I suspect, you're welcome to stay in it free of charge till you're finished."

I could tell Joe was getting restless because he'd started shifting his weight from one foot to the other while vigorously plowing his hand through his hair.

"Aunt Polly's funeral is tomorrow at eleven-thirty. Service will be at Swinnforth-Morris Mortuary." He pointed back the way we'd traveled earlier in the day as he sketched a path in the air. "Up the street and over two blocks. Come to the funeral. I want you to meet the people you'll be working with if we come to an agreement. Carrying things. Doing whatever you want done."

"Thanks, I'll stay in the apartment overnight while I work up a proposal for the particulars of this job."

Joe handed me two keys, one to the apartment, the other to the main house. "Gotta' go," he said. "People to see, places to be." Like the wind, he and Sparky made tracks down the driveway to his Cadillac.

7

NOSY ME, I COULDN"T RESIST looking through one of the dirty garage windows before going upstairs to the apartment. It was dark inside but I could make out a workbench along the back wall and two large shapes, both under yellow tarps. From their different sizes I thought they probably covered a truck and a car. A set of steps in a back corner most likely led to the apartment.

I went around to the back of the building and climbed the wide wooden outside stairs to the apartment over the garage. Turning the key, I pushed open the door. An agreeable smell of fresh paint and recently cut wood swirled around me as I entered.

The quarters looked exactly like Joe had described. A bright yellow mini-kitchen held a small stove and a half-sized refrigerator. One of the tiniest microwave ovens I've ever seen sat along side a dinky sink. The beige vinyl flooring needed a good scrubbing. I opened the wall cupboards on either side of the window over the sink. Inside I found everyday dishes, pots, pans, a crockpot, and an appliance indispensable to my mornings, a Mr. Coffee.

The all-purpose room had a small wooden kitchen table covered with a blue and white plaid tablecloth. Two metal folding chairs leaned against the wall. The table had been placed just around the corner from the kitchen door to make a tiny eating alcove. In another corner of the room sat a gray metal, army-issue desk, with a wooden fold-up chair open in the kneehole. A heavy-duty couch, upholstered in neutral plaids, was probably a foldaway bed. It sat along one wall facing a large picture window. A convenient lamp with a 150-watt bulb screwed into place was on a small table within easy reading distance from the end of the couch. The floor covering of low pile, dark green carpeting looked new. Cream-colored paint covered the walls. In the middle of the back wall I noticed a door that in all probability led down a stairway to the garage.

The bedroom had a masculine feel. The double bed and chest of drawers had been painted a deep, dark brown. In the right-hand corner a large cocoa-colored leather recliner with a generic table and lamp sat next to it, taking up a major part of the room. The floor was covered in a dark brown shag rug. *Boring!* Instinctively I wondered how light beige curtains and a bright multi-colored rag rug would look in here. A tiny bathroom near the bed held a shower, stool, and a small sink.

I went back to the living area and saw a cast-iron doorstop conveniently standing along the baseboard, so I used it to prop open the door for fresh air. The doorstop depicted three painted marching geese. What I remembered, from an antique price guide, was that the piece had been called a door porter in the past, and produced in this country sometime after the Civil War. I personally had seen several of this type and knew it to be worth over five hundred dollars. Of course, the prices for antiques range from high to low depending on the condition of any given piece. I thought that the Hubley Company had probably produced this door porter but would have to look that up to be sure.

Much like our forefathers had been called "hunters and gatherers," Mother and I hunted and gathered in antique shops when I was a little girl. We periodically made the rounds of all the local stores in Peoria. After I started my family and on my days off at the hospital where I worked as an ER nurse, I went antique hunting from those same stores. There is an unknown something I can't identify that satisfies my soul when I resurrect some old forgotten piece. If I discover a treasure in some little out of the way place I give it new life by making it mine.

I needed to begin work on an inventory sheet and come up with estimates for Joe about the work to be done. I pushed aside a stack of newspapers from one corner of the desk. I was curious, so reached and turned the pile over. The top paper was dated October 22 of this year. The article told the story of a possible homicide in Carterville on the day before Miss Carter had died.

> *At approximately 8:30 p.m. yesterday,
> Carterville residents wondered what was
> happening when many citizens received calls
> from the Fulton County Sheriff's office telling
> them to stay in their homes with the doors
> locked. According to a spokesman, a 911 call
> had been received from a person claiming to
> have shot a man. The call was garbled, but the
> caller said, "I just shot someone." All 911 calls
> are investigated immediately and officers went
> to the address identified. The police searched
> the house, which appeared to be empty. The
> search was terminated around midnight and an
> all clear issued after the phone call appeared
> to be false. The caller has not been found.*

I wondered what that was all about and thought I'd ask someone later.

To save myself a bundle of money, I decided to take Joe up on his offer to stay in the carriage apartment. After his aunt's funeral I'd have made up my mind as to whether I could even handle a job this daunting.

It was late afternoon and I was hungry. I also needed to pick up my gear from the motel. Joe and I had looked through the house for hours and the go-power of the sugar-charged donut I'd eaten early this morning had long since disappeared.

If I were Gretel of fairy tale fame I would have sprinkled crumbs along the way as I followed Joe here so I could find my way back to town—and to food. I left the apartment and meandered down the driveway to the street to get into my car. Reversing directions, I found my way back to town. The number on the Carter house porch was 1200. The name of the street—no stretch of my imagination—was Carter.

Carterville's main downtown business establishments appeared to be about four blocks long and maybe two blocks deep. I couldn't see a grocery store sign so thought that in all probability people living here traveled to a larger town to buy provisions, maybe Canton, Lewistown, Pekin, or Peoria.

My first stop was at a service station on Main Street. Ron (printed in block letters with a black marker on his faded yellow shirt pocket) came over all set to gas up my car.

"I don't need any gas right now," I told him. "I'm new in the neighborhood. All I want is a map of Carterville."

Without delay Ron underwhelmed me as he tried to prove a superior intellect. He attempted to examine the contents of my brain, probing for information about why I was here in Carterville. My chin elevated and my "Granite-head" inclination took over. I refuse to be bullied, and have never in my life liked getting the third degree. I particularly dislike gossip. I knew Ron was most likely searching for tittle-tattle to entertain his buddies.

I smiled at him and softly asked, "Are you with the visitor police?"

He stared at me, his shifty green eyes narrowing. His chin dropped to his chest, the action pulled his mouth open.

It stayed that way while I informed him, "Go to whomever it is that you share gossip with and tell them you didn't learn anything from me."

I reached over with my index finger, placed it gently under Ron's chin, and pressed upward, effectively closing his mouth.

Jumping into my car, I zoomed away from the station but could see Ron in the rearview mirror. He was shaking his head like it was full of bees.

I've had years of practice at being a clam and was much better at it than Ron was at digging out information. Experience has taught me that letting any cat out of the bag is a whole lot easier than putting one back in.

Ron, in all probability, never lets an inquiry opportunity go untested.

My junk food radar has been honed to precision over the years. I spied the colors of a Subway shop a block away and drove over, parked, and zipped into the tacky little building. The wallpaper was in keeping with the corporate theme of black-and-white scenes of a New York Subway plastered on the walls.

I opened the door to the restorative smells of bread baking and cholesterol, nitrate-loaded luncheon meat. I started my pursuit of a sandwich at the far end of the counter. Subway shops won't allow you to start in the middle, not even if you're the only customer in there. I tried it a few times but was never successful. The older I get the longer my list becomes of items I think are not worth the trouble of lining up for. Junk food is not on that list.

Two female customers sat at the table by the front window eating as they looked out at a view of the empty Main Street. One man was giving his order. My conditioned brain propelled me, in the approved manner, opposite the cash register. My turn at last! I gave my order to a young girl who looked like an anorexic mosquito. I'd bet she never ate here.

"I'll have a foot-long BMT," I told her. When I first started craving that particular sandwich I asked what the initials stood for. I was told they mean Biggest, Meatiest, and Tastiest. I continued with my order, "Make that on white Italian bread with provolone cheese, Genoa salami, pepperoni, ham, lettuce, tomatoes, onion, black olives, light on the Jalapeño peppers, double mayo and yellow mustard, oil and vinegar, salt and pepper." By then I was out of breath and salivating like Pavlov's dog at a training session.

After I paid for my food I left the shop while considering the pros and cons of eating half of it now and saving the other half for breakfast. I sat in my car and gobbled down the first half as I made happy "Ummm, Ummm, good," sounds.

After I ate I wanted to get a sense of the town so strolled up Main Street in Carterville's sad-looking downtown area.

The exteriors on the wooden one-story decaying buildings had all turned 'Illinois-weather' gray. They looked as though they might be a hundred years old with only one exception, the red brick, two-story Carterville Bank on the corner. I wandered past a restaurant, Grandma's Place, a five-and-dime, a laundry, and another shop, Susie's Used Clothing. Benny's Pool Hall caught my eye and I heard a familiar click of one ball contacting another as I walked past. Old recognizable smells of stale beer and cigarette smoke floated out the open door. Playing pool was my favorite pastime as a skip school tomboy. I still like to play eight ball when I have the time to spare. I turned a corner, walked a block and came down a secondary street named First Avenue. Art work, crafts, and antique shops leaned on one another. Their windows displayed dusty objects in an attempt to lure customers inside. There wasn't a cat or dog to be seen and the street held one pedestrian. Me!

A sign pointing to Route 24 was on the corner, so I walked back to my car then followed its direction. The Sleep Inn motel came into sight as I rounded the first curve. I parked and entered the Blue Room and packed my meager belongings. When I went to check out, I reminded the clerk to put the room charge on Joe Carter's tab.

He snickered and rolled his eyes as if trying to look at the top of his head. He must have thought putting a room charge on Joe's bill was as amusing and unusual as I did?

I shoved the blue ping-pong paddle key across the counter at him, left the office and drove to the pay phone I'd seen outside the Subway shop on Main Street. I closeted myself in the cubbyhole of glass and ripped the map of Carterville from the back section of the phone book. I looked it over then found my way back to Carter Street.

Turning in the driveway, I drove in, parked, took my overnight case from the trunk and climbed the back stairs to the apartment. I unpacked my insufficient wardrobe and settled in.

It was time to work up a proposal for Joe, so I sat down at the desk and organized my paperwork. I brought with me a many-paged contract designed to take care of the legalities of this job. There were numerous heretofores and whereases I didn't attempt to understand. Filling in all of the blanks, I made this a four-week commitment and threw in an option for either of us being able to change our minds.

I took a break and went to the picture window to gawk outdoors. I could see the main house and could look through the windows of the second floor room where Polly had lived. With illumination from the few rays of a harvest moon filtering through the trees, I saw the section missing from the widow's walk with that little piece of yellow tape fluttering.

In the kitchen I ate the remaining half of my sandwich. Now I'd have to find a place to eat in the morning since I'd already polished off my breakfast. Maybe I'd try that Grandma's Place I'd seen downtown. I went back to the desk and worked out more details about how I would be able to pull off this appraisal.

Establishing my fee, I spelled out the fact that I was to be allowed to live in the apartment at no cost to me. In the event that something unexpected came up during the first four weeks, Joe and I could renegotiate any issue. By the time I finished the paperwork I had an eight-page contract that I hoped covered everything important.

Wedging the two kitchen chairs under the doorknobs of both doors. I leaned cooking pots on the seats of each, then placed drinking glasses in them. Need is vital for invention. This would be an alert signal if someone tried to enter. Next time I went to Peoria I intended to bring my non-electric burglar alarm from home.

I set Big Ben for nine a.m. Cranked up the heat. Crawled under the covers. Slept like the proverbial inert log.

8

THE ALARM HADN'T SOUNDED. I woke up at 10:30. Double damn it! I'd forgotten to pull out the button on Big Ben. Now I'd have to hustle if I wanted to get to Ms. Polly's funeral service on time. I showered, and dressed in the black suit I'd worn last night to Foggy Bottom. I was torn between two choices for footwear, red alligator heels or the Reeboks. I knew wearing red shoes to a funeral would be tacky. My options were red high heels, tennis shoes or go barefoot. The red heels it would be.

If I intended to stay in Carterville any length of time I'd have to make a run home and bring back some clothing changes. I also needed to fill Venus in on what was happening, check up on my business, and of course find out how my cat Sugar was doing.

It was eleven and I'd be late if I delayed much longer. I hurried out the door and down the stairs. Incorrectly dressed as usual, I drove to the funeral.

The small sign, perched on a white picket fence, read Swinnforth-Morris Mortuary. I parked between a red van and a blue pickup in the visitor section and rushed up the concrete walk to the building. Turning the faux-gold knob on the door, I pushed it open. It inched inward with a slow, low, swooshing sound as it traveled over thick, beige carpeting. Somber soft music surrounded me as I entered. It seemed to come from in-between the walls.

I looked up, up, up, at a beefy grim-faced man who was looking at the top of my head. I immediately felt like I'd done something grossly wrong. With distaste as evident as the outsized nose on his face he furrowed his brow. Then frowned at my red high-heeled shoes. I scrunched my toes up and felt like clicking my heels together, like Dorothy's, "There's no place like home" from *The Wizard of Oz*.

A somber bass voice like Lurch on the Addams Family TV show rumbled, "I'm Mr. Morris." The words hovered above my head. Mr. Morris steered me into the "Eternity Room" where Miss Carter's body lay in a glossy mahogany coffin. Mr. Morris led me to the casket. I looked down at Polly Carter's remains, lying on shiny white satin. Pearls, powder, and snow-white hair summed up my quick impression.

I wondered if a recluse would want to be placed on exhibit like this. Probably not.

Big city funerals are now being offered with a framed glossy photograph of the smiling departed one. The picture of the deceased is usually placed right next to a grim reminder of, "ashes to ashes, dust to dust," gathered in an urn. I think the scheme of calling these funerals

"A celebration of life" was meant to generate an upbeat atmosphere.

I'll take an old-fashioned memorial service any day. They were designed with the mourner in mind as an occasion to have one last look at the loved one, and to cry, while saying a final goodbye.

Small towns like Carterville still hold open viewing of the departed, the top half of the body showing, decked out in finery. They, poor souls, looked like they'd been shoehorned into the casket or like a man's handkerchief in the breast pocket of a suit coat.

Cookie cutter pallbearers had lined up along one wall waiting to carry Polly's earthly remains out to a hearse, then to a pre-arranged final resting place in a soon to be forgotten cemetery.

Joe had told me his Aunt Polly Carter had no family members alive except him. I couldn't detect a wet eye in the place. The only information I knew about Miss Carter was that she gradually withdrew from society and isolated herself in her home these past forty years. I wondered what happened to cause her to turn her back on all relationships, except the ones with her nephew and the caregiver. She looked so vital in that portrait at the Carter House. *How sad!*

When I was very young I thought the rhetoric heard at funerals was meant to deceive visitors into thinking the departed one had left the building but was expected to return soon.

My parents knew many people from dissimilar denominations. When I was six I heard a minister say my Aunt Shelby was one of those dearly departed ones. I thought she'd gone grocery shopping at the Piggly-Wiggly, or maybe over to Main street to visit her sister, my Aunt Marge. I asked father where Aunt Shelby had gone. He picked me up and pointed at her lying flat on white satin in a big shiny wooden box. In my father's arms the new viewing position allowed me to see her. She was stretched out, dressed in her finest, and looked like she was taking a nap.

I wondered back then why the dead clutched something to take with them into eternity. Since then I've been to many funerals and seen lifeless hands holding a Bible, a rosary, a pair of reading glasses, a lily. One especially sad time I saw a child grasping a stuffed bear in her small lifeless hands that lay on her motionless chest.

I thought, years ago, the dead were taking a gift to God, or it was something for them to while away their time when they arrived in that unknown place, Eternity. Death was a mystery to me.

Once, I asked Aunt Shelby, "If God forgets to guard me from dying, what will happen?"

She told me, "I know two things you can do. You can choose which you want to use."

I was excited to think there was a different way to protect myself if God happened to have an off day.

Aunt Shelby said, "You can string some garlic to wear around your neck, or I can teach you to pinch salt."

Ick. I hated the smell of garlic so went for the salt pinch.

"What you do, Annie, is this. Take a smidgen of salt and fling it over your shoulder and say, 'Save me. Save me.'"

After I made a large dent in mother's stockpile of salt, it put a period to my "save me" routine.

I stopped asking people religious questions when I noticed them looking at me like I had two heads.

9

I LOOKED UP AND SAW JOE doing a rolling motion with his hand that apparently meant, "Come here."

As I approached, Joe took my arm and tugged, positioning me next to him. He introduced me to townspeople who had been surrounding him. I saw that Ron, the purveyor of news from the gas station, was in the group. I'd heard Ron whispering earlier to a collection of his cronies. Two words had escaped from his sibilant sound. I plainly heard "visitor police." I knew he was revealing the tale about his run-in with me yesterday. No doubt his gossip antenna twitched fast and furiously today. He was dressed for work and I thought, uncharitably, that there was probably nothing under his purple ball cap but hair. I wondered if Mr. Morris had looked down his sizable nose at Ron when he entered the mortuary wearing oily jeans and a grungy work shirt, like he'd frowned at my red shoes.

Joe began talking and everyone listened quietly. He began the tale about his Aunt's reclusive behavior. "What I've been told is that Aunt Polly began acting 'funny'

59

when she was in her late teens. She could often be heard muttering the same phrases over and over. Her mother noticed she'd developed a bizarre tendency to count various objects repetitively. Polly's twentieth birthday was on December 24. She was making plans to marry her sweetheart on Valentine's Day the next year."

"Her fiancé, Harry Cody, had given her a magnificent diamond necklace as a betrothal/Christmas present. Before they could marry her peculiar condition deteriorated further. Her sweetheart jilted her. Left town. Aunt Polly never heard from him again."

Joe turned his head and looked at his aunt with a sad face, sighed, then continued. "Through the years Polly's parents sought a cure from several physicians for her abnormal behavior. As a last procedure, after a long line of trials and errors, her doctors tried passing huge currents of electrical energy through her body—known today as electro-convulsive therapy. Nothing worked. Then Aunt Polly became physically cruel and would assault those who cared for her."

Joe plowed a hand through his hair, gave a big sigh, and went on to finish his aunt's story. "Polly's parents, years ago, set up a trust fund that would take care of her for life. Aunt Polly has never had to worry about everyday necessities of life, like paying rent or buying groceries. That was all automatically taken care of for her through the bank. Finally, her odd behavior caused her to disassociate from people and everyday life. Her father died in Sedalia, Missouri when she was in her twenties. When she was fifty her mother was killed in an automobile accident. A semi demolished the car she was driving on Highway 24, a mile before the Foggy Bottom turnoff. After her mother died, Aunt Polly was left alone in that big old house.

"Mrs. B answered an ad that Polly's trustees ran in the paper searching for a full-time caregiver. They hired her. She has devoted years of her life taking care of my aunt, who never again left her home. She became more and more reclusive in the last stages of her illness. Finally, in her last years Aunt Polly wouldn't even leave her room."

10

AS A NURSE WITH YEARS of experience, I recognized the mental confusion of an obsessive-compulsive disorder, OCD. Years ago, if a person showed signs of OCD they would be stigmatized and not properly treated. One out of fifty people today is afflicted with obsessive-compulsive disorder to varying degrees. I remember those numbers readily because I had a neighbor diagnosed with the same thing, and I dug into research it at that time.

It seems the cause of OCD comes from deep within the brain and originates in a structure there called the striatum. The striatum is made up of two parts, and each of those parts relies on a mass of nerve cells involved in processing messages coming from other parts of the brain. The striatum is concerned with sensory information. It's somewhat like, when a normal person sees a speck of dirt on the floor, that visualization is then translated, without having to think about it, into body movements to pick up that speck. In OCD, the filtering mechanism has become faulty. Instead of picking up the speck, obsessive movements like rubbing the hands together or repeating phrases or any number of bizarre behaviors can be the end result. That behavior, in effect, will take the place of the normal action of simply bending over and picking up the speck.

The crowd around Joe scattered after he finished telling his account of Polly's life. I took the opportunity to ask, "Will you come by the carriage house later tonight, Joe, to look over my proposal? If it meets with your approval, I can start working next week."

"Sure, I can. How about five, Annie?"

"Okay by me," I said and did some woolgathering and wall-leaning at the back of the room.

When I looked up again I saw Joe coming toward me escorting an elderly lady I'd noticed earlier. He introduced her as Mrs. Bagley, his Aunt Polly's caregiver. She looked to be in her seventies and had been the one to find Polly's body.

Mrs. Bagley was built sturdily with skinny long limbs. Her feet were turned out in an awkward, splayfooted stride. Her thinning gray hair worn in short spiky tufts, framed a drawn February face. Sad blue eyes gave a lie to the smile she wore. I thought she most likely would be a valuable person to get to know if I had questions about Polly's personal effects. Maybe she was the one and only true mourner here. She and Miss Carter had a history of years behind them. The two had grown old together.

Mrs. Bagley was a welcome change. She was talkative and didn't seem to mind sharing information. We shook hands and she told me to call her by the same name everyone in town did, Mrs. B. She seemed to want to talk about finding Miss Carter's body.

I'd assumed the fall that took Polly's life had happened somewhere in the house. Mrs. B told me that Polly had fallen from the widow's walk. Then I remembered seeing the broken wooden railing on the roof with that little piece of yellow tape clinging to it. I wondered why Joe hadn't said something to me about where she'd fallen from the day she died.

"It challenges my imagination," said Mrs. B, to think of that poor old frail woman. She could hardly walk, let alone climb those metal twisty stairs to get up to the roof. Just doesn't make sense to me." She wiped her eyes before continuing.

"I told the police I hadn't known Polly to attempt stairs for the past fifteen years. She had me to fetch and carry for her. Never left her bedroom. I tucked her in every night at eight. She never needed me until the next morning. That was our agreement, eight to eight. I always made sure her commode was by the bed. She transferred on and off without a problem. With a pitcher of water and a glass handy on her bedside table she'd be set for the night."

I found myself making commiserating sounds, "Uhhm, hmmm," and the ever popular "Ohhh," with raised eyebrows and a brief nod while Mrs. B unloaded her troubled mind.

The lights in the room dimmed. The organ music ended. Everyone scurried to his or her chosen chair. Mrs. B fluttered a work-worn hand at me and said, "Gotta' go now. See you later." She walked to the front of the room and sat beside Joe in the front row. It was so quiet in my area I could hear the people around me breathing in and out, in and out.

The minister took his customary place front and center at a small podium bedecked with a large spray of gladioluses. As a signal that he was ready to talk he cleared his throat noisily. With his white clerical collar and black suit I thought he had the look of a young Bing Crosby when he played the role of a Catholic priest in the old movie, "The Bells of St. Mary's." The sermon was short and seemed to be a generic kind of a script. One size fits all.

Less than fifteen minutes after the service started it was over. Everyone left the building and began jockeying for placement behind the black hearse that was to carry Polly's remains to the cemetery. Joe helped Mrs. B enter his Cadillac, and everyone else lined up in his or her vehicles behind the hearse.

I saw Ron jump up into the driver's side of a truck. Most of it the basic dull pale gray color of Bondo, a substance used to patch holes in the metal of vehicles. He maneuvered his truck to the front of the line-up, positioning it behind Joe's car. He sure had brass balls. Dusty trucks, vans, jeeps, and cars in various states of repair—and disrepair—lined up behind Ron's truck. Everyone was talking and laughing inappropriately. It seemed more 'party time' than a funeral.

I opted not to go to the cemetery. Instead, I drove around in search of food. I hadn't eaten breakfast and my backbone had been saying hello to my belly button this past hour. I drove to Main Street and pulled into the gravel parking lot at the side of the ratty looking restaurant I'd seen yesterday in Carterville. Hand-printed letters on the front window in watered down red stated "Grandma's Place." I went inside and slid onto a stool at the counter. I came face to face with Grandma. She was working the grill.

Grandma was maybe four and a half feet tall and held a burger flipper in her right hand. A lit cigarette with an inch long ash nestled in the right corner of her bluish-purple lips. A chore-girl-looking hairdo rode on top of her head over a face the color and texture of a dried apple. Her long skinny nose almost touched her chin. I could barely discern the black color of shoe-button eyes that had nearly disappeared among the wrinkles. Her white apron was decorated with several weeks' worth of dried on food. Grandma looked like a tied-in-the-middle, unhygienic potato sack.

The menu offered the usual fare found in any restaurant across the country. Printed on a scrap of paper and attached with a paper clip were three additional delicacies, red-eye gravy, grits, and fried green tomatoes.

Those items were probably an essential food group here in Carterville. I thought, what the hell, live it up, and ordered all three, along with one egg over easy and a buttermilk biscuit.

When the food arrived, the bowl of grits had no flavor, so I poured the red-eye gravy over the mess, then sopped fried green tomatoes in the grit soup I'd produced. Maybe I was extra hungry but I thought it was lip-smacking good.

Grandma stared at me while I made the grit soup as if I was committing a criminal act. I turned my lips up at the corners in a facsimile of a smile. She didn't smile back. At least I don't think she did. If I read the expression on her face correctly, she was no doubt wondering if I came from another planet. Since I was the only customer in the place and Grandma wasn't the least bit chatty I didn't linger. I paid my bill and went back to the apartment.

When Joe arrived I offered him coffee that he turned down. I went to the desk, picked up my proposal and handed it to him. He flipped through it and made some uh huh, yep, and hmmm sounds. I told him if he found the proposal satisfactory that I intended to go to Peoria in the morning to check on my business, and bring back some equipment I needed for this job.

Joe didn't ask any questions about the proposal. He signed his name on the dotted line, and wrote a good faith check. I officially would start working at Carter house this Wednesday a.m.

After Joe left I did another McMuffit happy dance.

11

ON MY WAY BACK TO PEORIA the next morning I mulled over my to-do list.

#1-Deposit Joe's check and pay delinquent bills

#2-Set up Venus's work schedule

#3-Pack for the trip back to Carterville tomorrow

#4-Set up a system for inventory at Joe's place

#5-Talk baby talk to Sugar so she'll know I hadn't abandoned her

Thinking about my cat prompted me to remember the day she'd adopted me. There had been a driving rain all day. My business is typically made up of walk-by customers. No sales are generated in foul weather. I closed early and went home.

Letting myself into the house, I picked up, pointed, and clicked the remote at the television and heard a strange noise. At first I thought it came from the TV. The odd racket increased to a compelling level. I traced the sound to the front door. I looked through the security peephole. No one was standing on the porch. I unlocked the door and eased it open to a full-grown waterlogged cat. The thing zoomed in. Its long skinny tail, stiffly erect with a crook at the top, made it look like a question mark as the cat sprinted away. It disappeared behind the sofa.

I coaxed the wet thing from behind the couch with "Here, kitty, kitty." When I looked into its two, big, beautiful baby blue eyes, I decided to take in a cat resident if no one claimed it.

The cat lay compliant at my feet and let me sop water from its skinny body. I observed no untidy male parts cluttering up the spot between its back legs. A female variety! I dubbed it "Sugar" because it had snow white hair, then decided to humanize it and called the cat "her" instead of "it." Scratching behind her ears prompted a rumbling that vibrated her body. Sugar trotted to the kitchen, sat down in front of the refrigerator, and stared up at it. Then she looked back at me, looked again at the refrigerator. She repeated those moves several times, till I got the message, "I'm hungry," in unspoken cat language. I decided that Sugar must have exceptional feline intelligence.

After drinking a cup of milk from a cereal bowl in a dainty catty way she began a personal hygiene routine. She licked her paw, then ran that damp paw behind her ears and over her face and down her whiskers. When she finished cleaning her face and whiskers she shot one of her back legs straight up in the air then bent in a damned uncomfortable-looking position and groomed her nether region. After that spurt of cleanliness, she made a beeline to the living room, and launched herself onto the navy blue cloth recliner that I call my command center. Sugar had dried and fluffed out. She'd been blessed with exceptionally long hair, a substantial amount of which quickly relocated onto my chair.

I snapped my fingers and commanded, "Down," in a firm voice pointing to the floor in a pathetic attempt to get the cat out of my chair. Sugar had her own ideas. Wide blue eyes blinked up at me. She circled several times then curled up in a spherical, puffed-up, ball of white fur. The cat instantly went from active to dormant. I sat on the couch.

I adopted Sugar. I'm an easy mark that animals seem to sense.

* * *

I arrived at Annie's Attic at 9:15 the next morning, pleased to find that good old reliable Venus had opened the store. So much had happened in Carterville these past three days that when I got back to my shop in Peoria, I felt like I'd been gone for a month.

Last year Venus folded a catering business she'd started two years ago called "The Foodie." She's so soft hearted that she gave away more food than she charged for. Her business slowly went belly up, so she filed in bankruptcy court. We often talked about the risks of owning your own business, and about my shop being in the red far too long. I was hoping, with the advent of Joe, I could turn things around.

I thought Venus might have learned her lesson with that catering business going broke, but oh no, she said she was saving money to open a different business. She wouldn't tell me what kind. One can only imagine.

Last month at the shop I walked up on her suddenly and she quickly flipped over a book she'd avidly been reading. I'd seen her engrossed in that book the previous week. Its focus was on interior, architectural, and landscape designs. *Feng Shui!* The book was about the art of furniture arranging according to an Eastern tradition. I asked her to tell me about it. She went way over my head with details. She talked about how crystal, wind chimes, table fountains, and mirrored balls benefit one's life, finances, and relationships.

Today when I entered Annie's Attic I sensed rather than saw a difference. Something about the place was off. I looked around the shop as Venus fairly glided out of the office to meet me, instead of her usual hustle-bustle. We hugged a greeting.

"What's different in here, Venus?"

She pointed to a row of mirrors on the wall, a gurgling fountain in a back corner by the office, several vases of flowers sitting at strange angles, and a wind chime that dangled over the door.

"We're reflecting, redirecting, and shifting energy in here." Venus said in a slow, hushed voice, not in her usual loud, fast, rambling way. "Sharp lines and corners are to be avoided. I've moved your desk so you have a clear line of sight to the door, and a good view of the display room. Now you should feel more relaxed with all of those things in proper alignment." Then she offered to "do over" my house.

She was really in to it.

12

OH, OH! FENG SHUI MALARKY! A giant sign blinked off and on in my head along with the repeating words, "SNAKE OIL, SNAKE OIL, SNAKE OIL."

Trying to change the subject I asked Venus to work full time these next four weeks. She readily agreed.

"How's Sugar, Venus?"

"Sugar's been missing you like crazy."

Venus cat-sat for me earlier this month and Sugar had to cope with an empty bowl after Venus forgot about her needs. Myrtle, my nosy-ass neighbor, thought I was mistreating the cat when she heard Sugar yowling for food. She turned me into the Animal Watch Society. I had a danged hard time convincing those people that Sugar hadn't been abused and the only thing wrong was her being spoiled rotten.

My neighbor, Mary, who lives in the house on the other side of mine, told me that Myrtle had lived there when she'd moved into hers twenty-five years ago. She also told me, "Myrtle is unique. Not everyone can make a mountain out of a molehill."

Myrtle is exceedingly opinionated, immediately voicing negative views on any topic. Her scruffy white hair is cut in a short bob and is straight as a stick. She's 70ish, thin, peewee-sized, and makes small hiccuppy movements with no noticeable purpose. Her little black beady eyes dart everywhere except at the person she's talking to. She could "piss off" a piss ant.

I've often wished Myrtle would move far, far away, preferably to a cannibalistic culture where they would stuff her scrawny little body into one of their ceremonial cooking pots.

Later that day I deposited Joe's check into the business account, wrote checks for the delinquent bills, and mailed them off. That felt good. Then I packed my car with several of my trusted *Antiques* price guides. I added supplies I would need in Carterville, my giant magnifying glass, a magnet to check out metal items, measuring tape, and numerous inventory sheets. Next I packed several changes of clothing in my suitcase for the coming week. I went back into the house, talked to Sugar, and promised her that Venus would keep her fed this time. I knew I would miss the cat far more than she would miss me.

After clearing up some paper work at the shop, I went to the grocery store and stocked up on half a dozen easy to do box mixes, some canned goods, coffee, and paper supplies to take with me. Then I left for Carterville.

I turned into the driveway and parked by the carriage house at ten-thirty. The bleak night turned black as licorice candy when I turned off the car lights. I took my six-battery flashlight from under the seat, clicked it on, tucked my non-electric alarm system under my arm, and grabbed my suitcase. The flashlight lit my speedy feet to the stairs in back of the building. Gusting wind tried to steal my breath. It wormed its way down my collar and up under the bottom of my jacket. The only sounds I heard were the complaining wind shrieking through the oak trees, the crunching sound my footsteps made traveling over the gravel, and my heart beating a rapid rhythm in my ears.

Because of the isolation of the apartment I'd decided I'd be more comfortable with my non-electric burglar alarm with me, exercising a bit of justifiable paranoia. I rushed up the back stairs leaving the car packed till morning's light. My homemade warning system consists of several sheets of one-inch plastic bubble wrap that I get from Mary, my next door neighbor in Peoria, whose husband owns a professional movers and storage business. How it works is this: I lay several sheets of bubble wrap in front of doors and windows then put any old throw rug on top of them. If I hear pow, pow, pow, the sounds bursting bubbles make when someone steps on them, it alerts me that someone has entered my zone. I laid one alarm in front of the door that I used as access to the apartment. Another, I placed in front of the door that led to the garage stairs.

Not sleepy yet. I began thinking about the two shapes I'd seen in the garage under the apartment. For something to do, I went to the stairway leading down to the garage and adjusted my alarm rug by the door so I wouldn't trigger it. I flipped on all the light switches I could find, unlocked the door, opened it, and looked into a black hole. No lights were on down there. I breathed easier when I noticed every light in the apartment had lit up. I looked at the wall alongside the small landing at the top of the stairs, and sure enough there were six switches. I flipped them all. The garage lit up like Christmas at Macy's, and down I went.

Ignoring the boxes and containers stacked helter-skelter I headed for the tarp covered shape that looked like it could be a car. I picked up one corner of the cover and there was no mistaking the shiny red color on a front fender of an automobile. I raised the tarp a little higher. A window came into view. I could see that the door lock was the same color as the interior. A major thought zinged through the clutter in my brain.

I ran back upstairs to use my cell phone and called my son-in-law, Frankie, who was "into" collectible cars. I told him that I thought I'd found a 1964 ½ Ford Mustang. He squeaked, then banged the receiver down in my ear, and went to look through his reference books about cars. I listened as he flipped through some pages, mumbling to himself. I couldn't have gotten much more excited than this and assumed, from the enthusiasm I heard in Frankie's voice, he must have felt the same way.

I kept Frankie on the line, took the cell phone with me, and went back down the stairs to the garage. After flipping the tarp completely off the car, I stood gazing at what I believed was a poppy red Ford Mustang. I remembered reading that their production had begun in March of 1964 and ended in August of that same year, explaining the half year. The Ford Mustang was the brainchild of Lee Iacocca, and designed by a racing-car driver named Carroll Shelby. The car had been a huge success with the public.

Frankie's voice sounded from the earpiece on the phone. "This book says there are a few items to check for authentication."

"Go ahead Frankie, I'm ready."

"The exterior gas cap should have no retaining wire."

I took the cap off and looked.

"Check," I said.

"The Mustang lettering on the front fenders should be 4-3/8 inches high."

I rushed over to the workbench and found a tape measure.

"Check," I repeated.

"Door locks will be color-keyed to the interior."

"Check."

"The front seatbelts need to be secured with an eyebolt."

"Check."

"The oil dipstick is located on the passenger side and is long."

"Check."

"The colors used on that model of Mustang were Phoenician yellow, tropical turquoise, champagne beige and poppy red."

"Check—the poppy red one."

This had to be a 1964 ½ mustang. Frankie told me that a car like this could be worth, in the neighborhood of twenty thousand dollars or more depending on what options were on it, and its condition. I thanked him over and over for the information he'd provided.

"No sweat, Ma," he said and hung up the phone.

When I looked at the odometer it registered only 178 miles. I was amazed that the upholstery showed no signs of mouse or other damage to the upholstery. I'd just earned my keep and then some.

I was tired, but went to the second shrouded shape and pulled off the tarp. It looked like pictures I'd seen of trucks carrying bootleg booze during prohibition. Oh! I sincerely hoped that's what it was. Then I spent too much time thinking—if it was a bootleg truck, what the hell was it doing here in Polly Carter's garage?

I'd have to look into it another time when I was perkier. I went back upstairs. It was midnight. I piled into bed, pulled the covers over my head, zoned out.

13

WEDNESDAY, EIGHT A.M. My first day on the job! Last night when I drove back to Carterville I'd decided to stay with my original plan and begin working in the attic. Joe and I hadn't taken the time to go there when we looked through the house on Sunday. I regard an attic as storage area, like mine in Peoria where I had a collection of junk from past years. I didn't expect any surprises up there.

My long-range plan was to keep separate inventory sheets for the furniture in the house and leave the heavy pieces where they sat. Next I'd stack the items with a value over fifty dollars along the wall on the right side of each room, for the auction. Joe could deal with the auctioneer when it came time for the sale. I'd shift the items worth less than fifty dollars to an empty space I'd seen in the garage when I uncovered the Mustang. This was going to be the granddaddy of all auctions and later a huge garage sale. I needed to advertise the estate auction in the Canton, Lewiston, Pekin and Peoria newspapers. I'd also run an ad in weekly papers in the many small towns within a fifty-mile radius of Carterville.

I ate a little cold cereal while wishing for a bowl of Grandma's hot grits and red-eye gravy, then I dressed. On my last birthday, my friend Nancy gave me the T-shirt I decided to wear today, which reads, "If you're a born again do you have two belly buttons?" I chuckle every time I read it.

When I entered the front door of the Carter house I walked over and stood in my "rainbow." The early morning sun shining through the dirty stained glass transom sent muted sparkles dancing around the front hall. I intended to clean that transom sometime later just to see if wiping away years of accumulated grime would generate a brighter display.

Mrs. B conveniently lives next door to the Carter house. Joe told me when we firmed up our contract that she would come over every noon Monday through Friday to fix my lunch. If I had any odd jobs, Mrs. B would help with those at his expense. Joe also said that if I needed a handyman I should ask Mrs. B to have her husband Willie come and do the chore. He hired Ron too, for moving any heavy items, and trash burning at the end of his shift at the gas station after three p.m. on Mondays, Wednesdays and Fridays. Joe was to pay all of them and told me not to worry about it. *A good deal for me!*

As I made my way up the curved staircase to the second floor to check out the family bedrooms, I noticed two worn trails in the muted colors of the paisley carpet runner on the stairs. Mrs. B must have made those tracks from her many years traveling up and down while tending to Polly Carter's needs.

There were six doors on the second floor. Three located on either side of the main hallway. Joe said his aunt's space had been expanded years ago by knocking down two of the walls, and combining three rooms.

A huge, ugly, unmade four-poster walnut bed had a dusty, moth-eaten purple velvet canopy above it. The eyesore dominated Aunt Polly's living space. The bed had been positioned so its occupant could look through the window for a view of the outdoors. When I looked through the window, and straight across, I could see into the all-purpose living room at the carriage house apartment. Next to the bed sat a commode and an oak table with metal claw feet. It held an odd assortment of items that must have been used by Joe's Aunt Polly.

Inside the room were three oak armoires standing in a row along one wall, like soldiers at attention. An old-fashioned wooden dressing table with a three-way mirror, its top covered with a lacy runner, was situated along another wall. A jumble of spilled powder, costume jewelry, white hairnets, and fancy crocheted gloves littered half of its top. A large assortment of glass perfume bottles that were creating a disgusting mingle of odors sat at the other end. Catty-cornered, facing the hall door, was a stained, maroon wing chair with tufts of cotton escaping its seams. A drop-leaf table sitting next to the chair held what appeared to be a gorgeous Tiffany lamp. Evidence of a burn was still in the fireplace. A short door, maybe four-feet high, was on the south wall. I swung it open. An ornate circular iron staircase came into view. Most likely this space was the entrance to the widow's walk I'd seen from the carriage house apartment. I wanted to explore up there when I had free time.

Houses built in the Victorian era had small rooms when compared to the current oversized ones. None of these bedrooms had a built-in closet. In the 1800s the number of rooms in a house determined the dollar amount of real estate taxes levied on the owner. Closets had been counted as rooms in that time period. They were taxed as such, creating an incentive for people to leave them out of design plans. Armoires were often used instead of closets to hold garments.

Wandering out into the hall again I saw the bare wood flight of stairs leading to the third floor. These weren't rich looking like the main staircase had been. They had no carpet covering. Pine had been used to build them instead of pricey oak. The steps sagged in the middle, groaning and complaining with squeaks and creaks under my weight. I made my way up the steep stairs and felt the handrail wobble, so determined it wasn't safe to use. I'd need to ask Mrs. B to have Willie work on it.

Climbing the stairs without using the banister, I arrived on the third floor. This area had probably housed the servants. In the era when this residence was built the domestic help, no doubt, doubled or tripled up in these tiny airless rooms. These quarters were piled high with miscellaneous clutter stacked any old way. Three boxy eight by ten rooms were located on one side of the hallway and two more on the other side. I opened a skinny door in the middle of the back wall and saw it only led down, probably servant's stairs. I trekked down and came out into the kitchen.

Going back up those same stairs to the third floor hallway, I maneuvered my way through the mess there to a narrow unpainted door at the far end of the back wall that most likely led to the attic. When I pulled that door open the inevitable squealing sounded. The house settling and the dried out hinges must have produced the eerie noise. Nevertheless, the hairs on the back of my neck and arms stood on end.

Taking a sizable gulp and a deep breath, I bolstered my courage. I climbed the steep, two-foot wide stairs knocking down cobwebs with my hands as I ascended. My head reached eye level with the floor of the attic. I could see two windows, one in front on the east wall, and another on the opposite west wall. A small thin strip of daylight bordered the edges of the window hangings that flipped and flapped as air patterns changed. A bare light bulb with a long string dangling from it clung to the middle rafter.

I cleared my throat at full volume. Then started talking out loud to myself, for encouragement. The loud voice was really meant to scare away any ghosts, mice, black widow spiders, or, God forbid, any one hundred foot-long snake living there. Well! Maybe a really large snake like those pythons I'd seen at the zoo. I especially do not like snakes.

When I fully emerged from the stairs into the attic I talked silliness rapidly at the top of my voice. I hurried to the light bulb. Yanked it. The string broke. It looped around my hand.

Less than a brilliant beginning in more ways than one. I went back down the servants' stairs to the main floor for string and a broom to arm myself in case I needed a scary critter weapon. I found a pair of scissors and a ball of new string in a junk drawer and cut off a sufficient length, then I grabbed a new light bulb. Back in the attic I pushed an old trunk underneath the burned out light fixture and crawled on top of it to attach the new piece of string. I pulled it. Nothing happened. The bulb was filthy and looked like it hadn't been changed in eons. I unscrewed it and inserted the new one. I pulled the string again and the light came on. Progress! I yanked down both ineffectual curtains. They looked as if they had once been a moth-eaten blanket torn in half, and nailed to the window frames.

Dang, that business of getting light up here to work by took over half an hour. I didn't have to punch a time clock working for Joe. Muley had always taught me to give an honest day's labor for my wages and I in turn taught that to my children. I carefully keep track of time spent. I'd work till five-thirty now then go to that Fall Harvest Festival tonight I'd seen advertised on posters around town. The announcements declared "The weather is cooling off and it's time for the 19th annual Arts and Crafts Festival at Carterville Community Park. There will be over fifty specially selected arts and crafts booths, a farmer's market, an international food court, a beer tent, and square dancing. The fun starts at 8 a.m. till 8 p.m. A Park N' Ride van will be available in front of the Shell station on Main Street."

The best thing of all—it's free. I really wanted to see what square dancing would be like here in Carterville. I'd been taking lessons in Peoria since my divorce last year but quit when I took this job. That kind of dancing is fun, and for a couch potato like me, who hates to exercise, square dancing became my fitness routine.

First things first though, work was primary on my agenda. I looked around the attic and decided to start culling in the southwest corner, then work my way around the perimeters until I reached the top of the stairs again. I unearthed two wooden folding chairs. One for me to sit on and one to hold a box of found articles to sort through.

The first box I chose was made of wood. It was so heavy I wound up pushing and pulling it to a space under the light bulb, but couldn't lift it onto the chair. The lid on the box was nailed shut. Again, I went down the stairs and out the back door to the garage workbench where I unearthed a claw hammer. In the attic once again I pried up the lid.

Little wonder I couldn't lift the box. It was full of cast iron banks. I picked up the top bank, wrapped in old newspapers. I removed the yellowed paper, flattened it out, and saw the eye-catching headlines about a shooting spree by the Cody gang in Peoria. I remembered hearing about them from Muley. When he'd been a young man, he said, three ruthless brothers who were bootleggers in Peoria and nearby counties had started the mob. The Cody gang increased to about fifty over the years and had run rampant.

The top bank was a mechanical bust of a clown. With a coin placed in its movable hand and a lever pulled, the hand moved up to the clown's mouth where a slot received it. The coin would then slip into the jester's mouth and disappear inside the bank. This was the very same bank that had been mass reproduced lately. The reproductions looked so real the public had been fooled into thinking them to be authentic. When I looked this bank over I could tell it was a bona fide antique. It was probably worth five thousand dollars, or more.

Who would have thought so many years ago that these banks purchased to save pennies, meant to amuse and promote thrift would escalate in price to such astronomical sums. Some mechanical banks can go for as much as five figures depending on the condition, rarity, and a final price determined between buyer and seller.

Under the clown wrapped in more newspapers lay another two banks. One, a Humpty-Dumpty figure sitting on a wall, the other was a replica of Charlie McCarthy perched on a trunk. I slipped an inventory sheet on my clipboard and started listing each bank as I removed it from the box. I had a total of thirty-three. When the box was empty I carried it to the wall on the north side of the attic where I'd assigned the auction items to be stockpiled. I carried the banks one by one, gently laying each back inside its box. I worked carefully so I didn't diminish their worth by chipping any paint.

I thoroughly enjoy the detective work it takes to authenticate an antique. The first lesson I learned from Mother years ago was how the definition of an antique had come about.

It seems that before the 1930s true antiques were considered to be duty-free, but the U.S. Customs Office needed to answer this one question repeatedly. What objects are classified as an antique? When they sought to clarify that question they came to the decision that an antique could be any object that pre-dated the mass production of the 1830s. Since that defining moment went back one hundred years, the Customs office declared that anything made over one hundred years ago could be considered an antique.

The beauty of their definition was in its flexibility. As the years moved forward so did the cut-off date justifying an antique's authenticity. The U.S. Customs Office then collected duty on anything younger than the century-old divider. The Customs Office still collects its revenue today using the same ruling. By having a set time limit of one hundred years the dealers and appraisers never have to try to convince a buyer that something is truly an antique.

Cast iron banks need to be looked at with knowledge when trying to determine if they meet the criteria for being a genuine antique. The earliest banks have to have parts that meet smooth and tight at the seams. The screws holding them together must have regular slotted screw-heads, not Phillips, keeping in mind that screws can be changed in anything. The paint on the banks should be matte rather than shiny. Old pieces often have patent marks on the inside so should be taken apart, or barring that, they should be looked at on the inside with a flashlight for any mark discernable. Genuine wear patterns are looked at with a magnifying glass. Irregular wear patterns mean the bank is a good quality, while back and forth marks indicate someone deliberately tried to make a new item look old.

If a piece has rust on it, old rust is brownish, new rust is orange. Reproductions are made from molds taken from an original. They are usually a bit smaller. Sizes for banks are given in antique books so I take my books and a tape measure with me. When I buy anything from a reliable seller I always ask for a "detailed" receipt of the item. Remembering the old saying, *"Let the buyer beware."*

I always say, "Let the buyer *be aware*." I do my homework!

14

MY WATCH READ ELEVEN o'clock though my rumbling stomach thought it should be noon, when Mrs. B was supposed to fix my lunch. There was still time to work another hour so I pulled a large cardboard box over to my work area beneath the light bulb. Inside the box I found yellowed, disintegrating papers dating back to the earlier years when Joe said the house had been built. A variety of books lay jumbled at the bottom. It looked like the box contained old household records, a new category I'd have to deal with later. I'd need to ask Joe what he wanted done with his family's personal papers.

I heard Mrs. B "Yoo-hooing" so went down to the kitchen by the servants' stairs and washed my hands at the sink. Expectantly, I sat down at the table in front of the place set for me. A tuna salad sandwich on rye, along with a bowl of vegetable soup and a cup of warmed-over breakfast coffee appeared in front of me. Yuck! Mrs. B, I could see, was not a gourmet cook. I don't like tuna for starters but picked at the sandwich. An empty can with a Campbell's red label lying in the garbage can confirmed my suspicion that the soup was not homemade. I pushed the rancid smelling coffee away untouched. I'd eat a bowl full of my primary snack of M and M's later.

Producing several loud forlorn sighs Mrs. B puttered around the kitchen. I didn't want to encourage a discourse, so kept silent. I wondered how long she could hold out before she filled me in on what was occupying her mind. After two minutes of quiet in the kitchen she finally turned to me, folded her hands over her ample front, and leaned her substantial backside on the edge of the sink. Mrs. B sucked in a huge breath, flared her nostrils and began a faultfinding monologue about her husband Willie's shortcomings.

"Annie, I'm fed up with my husband's behavior. That man was never, nor will he ever be, a ball of fire. That man's assigned only one job a day. That man didn't cut wood for the fireplace yesterday, like he'd been told to do."

I voiced a "hmmm." Then wondered if her husband answered to Willie or Thatman?

Like a runaway Peterbilt on a steep grade, Mrs. B continued her tirade. "The only time of the day he's awake is in between his naps. I asked him, 'Willie, if you don't do anything all day long, how will you ever know when you're done?' That man had a royal conniption fit. Said he'd never do a lick of work for me again. Well, humphh! I've heard that story before."

She definitely had been in the lead when pointy tongues were handed out. I did my usual with her, hmm hmmm, uh huh, and the raised eyebrows with an ohhh as emphasis. I'd never met Mr. B and wondered if he knew his wife informed people about his laid-back work habits.

Mrs. B, at long last, reached the end of her rant about Willie's shortcomings. I wasn't about to get involved in that volatile family squabble. I knew where my noon meals were coming from. I held onto the hope that tomorrow's lunch would be better.

I changed the subject.

"I haven't had time to organize any jobs for you yet Mrs. B, but will have a list of things ready this coming Monday afternoon." Then I took a deep breath and plowed ahead with a request for Willie to fix the wobbly stairway banister between the second and third floor.

"I'll tell him, Annie. Don't hold your breath waiting for that man. You just might turn blue before he shows up."

I remembered about wanting to ask her for information concerning the incident I'd read about in that newspaper over at the carriage house.

"Mrs. B, you found Polly when she died on the 22nd of this month, right?"

"That's right."

"I noticed an article in a newspaper over at the apartment about a happening in town on the evening before. It said an unknown caller dialed 911 and reported a possible homicide but it turned out to be a phony call. Do you know what part of town that took place in?"

"What's got you stirred up about that, Annie?"

"I'll be alone in the carriage house. I'm not easily frightened but do make every effort to stay out of harm's way."

"You can rest easy. That business all happened way over on the other side of town. Nothing came of it. Just a prank call. Gotta' go now and get gas in the car because that man didn't do it."

"Are you going to the station in town, Mrs. B?"

"Uh huh, it's the only one in Carterville."

"Will you tell Ron he doesn't need to come and burn trash till Monday after three?"

"I'll tell him, Annie, but he's such a nosy-poker, he'll probably come by anyway."

After lunch I trudged back up those three flights of stairs to the attic. I needed to organize my time in a more productive way so I wouldn't have to travel up and down those damned stairs so often.

Before I ate lunch I'd spied some decoys piled in the corner where I was keeping the over fifty dollar items for the auction. I thought I might as well start with them this afternoon and clear up more wall space. Decoys are appealing. They look so real and are an American art form. A. Elmer Crowell lived from 1862 to 1951, and his carved geese can go at auction for as high as six figures. A pair of mallard ducks by Charles Perdue, a noted Illinois decoy-maker, can be in the range of ten to twenty thousand dollars, again depending on condition. A high-quality decoy is one that's never been used.

I worked for two hours cataloging them on an inventory sheet and moved a few to the auction side of the room next to the box of banks, and some to the garage sale side of the room. I hadn't found any that were worth more than the one I thought might bring about five hundred dollars. Most of these decoys were pretty worthless, but could still be used as interior decorations. They'd seen a lot of river use. Shotgun marks had peppered them. Underneath the decoys I unearthed a flawless child's golden oak rocking chair with a caned back and seat. I carried it over and placed it on the auction side of the room.

After emptying three more boxes in the attic of garage sale items I shifted them to the left side of the room. Then stacked the junk next to the stairway, ready for Ron to carry down to burn on Monday.

At five-thirty I quit working for the day, went out the back door and locked the house. I let myself into the apartment and took a much-needed shower to wash off the dust and cobwebs. Slipping on a pair of clean jeans and a red sweater I grabbed my jacket and left for the Festival.

15

A DARK BLUE VAN that had a park-and-ride cardboard sign duct-taped to its front window pulled into the Shell station as I arrived. The van emptied its passengers so I hurried over and hopped on. I grabbed a seat behind the driver as some loud talkers clambered in filling the seats in back of me. The drone of their collective voices sounded like they were all talking at the same time. They were discussing what kind of food they would eat when they arrived at the Festival. The consensus seemed to be Chinese.

We traveled fifteen minutes to the Carterville Park, and the van pulled onto a filled-up gravel parking lot. When the driver opened the van's door everyone rushed out into a chilly evening of fall-nudging-winter. I inhaled one of my favorite scents at this time of year, burning leaves. At the Farmers Market, huge orange pumpkins were being judged to see who grew the largest one that year. The proud farmers milled around looking hopeful. Dried corn stalks, piled into shocks made the place extra festive. A large red-and-white overhead banner danced the wind and declared this to be

CARTERVILLE'S 19th ANNUAL FALL FESTIVAL

After that skimpy lunch Mrs. B served up, I immediately went to find the International Food Court. I was torn between Takee Outee, or Crepes. Takee Outee won. I ambled over and ordered a combination plate of Chicken Chop Suey, Fried Rice, and an Eggroll with sweet and hot mustard sauce. A short, thin, ancient Chinese man wearing a time-honored pigtail hanging far down his back took my order, then served me. He must have been a holdover from the traditions of old China because the braid concept had been gone from the Chinese culture here in the states many years. I thought I'd seen him going into the laundry next to the service station in Carterville yesterday, but by the time I'd done a double take he'd disappeared into the building.

The food here was surprisingly good. I munched while walking around, cleaned my plate, then dumped the used plastics and paper in a handy garbage can

I wandered up and down the arts and crafts aisle. Artists sat in tented stalls on fold-up chairs. This late in the day some of them still seemed optimistic about selling a painting of their interpretation of a local landscape. Vendors mingled with the crowd hawking crocheted doilies, painted wooden cutouts of tiny characters, handcrafted jewelry, you name it. In another tent a young woman was painting a pink heart on a little girl's face eliciting squeals of delight from cohorts who stood on the sidelines watching. I bought a shiny denim blue bracelet, "guaranteed to be Austrian crystal," I intended to wear with jeans. I like flashy sometimes.

A big red tent housed another main event of the night. Beer guzzling!

Familiar square dance music drifted in the air and lured me to the next tent. Onlookers stood around the perimeter of a temporary wooden floor. I'm built close to the ground so wriggled my way up to the front without sloshing any beer out of my mug. Six squares of couples stood in place, ready to dance a set, two songs played back-to-back. The music started and forty-eight people began whirling and twirling. Most of the time during my lessons back in Peoria there would be twenty-four, or three squares. By the large number of dancers I could see here, this must be a serious square dance town.

Piped out of Carterville's sound system, I heard the caller singing several old arrangements that I'd danced to in Peoria. Allemande left your Corner! Right and Left grand! Then this caller moved on to more advanced calls like, Flutter Wheel, Relay the Duecy, Spin, Change the Gears, All Eight Spin the Top, and my favorite to watch, Load the Boat.

The dancers looked like they were having such a good time my feet itched to join them. Then the caller started a singing call as the second one in the set that prompted everyone out on the dance floor to change partners. The routine was for a plus dance, much farther advanced than my group had been. I'd completed the beginner's class in Peoria and was halfway through their mainstream program.

I caught a glimpse of Joe on the dance floor. He wore cowboy boots and danced like his big feet were on fire. By the smile on his face stretching from ear to ear, I'd have to say he was having a really, really good time. He wasn't dancing John Travolta's style but he wasn't bad eye-candy for a man of his age. Joe partnered Monica from the Sleep Inn motel's Donut Hole. He sent Monica spinning around and around as she looked up into his face, laughing. Her enormous boobs bobbed up and down, around and around, nearly jumping out of her blouse.

These dancers were dressed in the required clothes of their club. The men wore white long-sleeved shirts and black pants with string ties. The women had on short, short, bright red bouffant skirts with stiff stand-alone lace slips, and ruffled petti-pants as underwear. As they swirled and twirled, the women looked like upside down tea cups spinning around.

When the music ended, the dancers on the floor yellow-rocked each other. One of the first things taught is that a "yellow rock," in square dance language, means a hug. When you hug another person you give them a valuable "nugget of gold." In other words a yellow rock.

I started walking toward the van to catch a ride back into town when Joe caught up with me. He tugged on my arm and turned me toward him.

"Do you square dance, Annie?"

"I do, but I'm a beginner. I'm halfway through mainstream lessons. You looked like you were having fun, Joe. I can't wait to get to the next phase so I can dance those complicated plus moves. I dropped out of class to do this job."

"This caller gives lessons on Thursday nights for your level. They're held at the Community Center's basement in town. There are always "angels" to help partner those who don't have one. Matter of fact I'm an angel. How about trying us out?"

"Maybe I will, thanks, Joe. By the way, I need you to look at some family papers I found in the attic. You can tell me what you want done with them."

"Be over in the morning after I finish fall plowing, Annie. About done with it. Couple of more hours should be all it takes."

"Okay, Joe."

With a wave of his hand he went back toward Monica and his dancing group, I walked away in the opposite direction. I looked back to see if he was looking back at me. He was.

The smile he gave me that time probably reached his denim blue eyes.

16

THE COLD NOVEMBER DAY dawned as I sat at the table thinking about how time seemed to be flying, but not me. At the rate I was sorting through Joe's newly acquired assets I'd be an antique myself. I had to pick up my rhythm.

Back at the Carter house, in the attic, I cleared a workspace under the bare light bulb where I could sit on the folding chair, then I dragged over a full cardboard box. It was a large size with paper towels stamped on its outside. The flaps over the top were folded over on each other but with a tug, they lifted easily. Dust flew everywhere.

Dolls rested inside. Some had been fashioned from porcelain and were called China dolls. A number were made of bisque and had realistic faces. One grungy-looking rag doll had shoe buttons for eyes.

What female, of any age, can resist cuddling a doll to her breast? I grabbed up a porcelain baby, cradled it in my arms, and gazed down into its glassy green eyes. I turned the doll over and searched its nape where the manufacturers place their symbols. These dolls were in good condition, except for the raggedy one. There were no cracks or chips evident to my naked eye. They were nicely dressed, with shoes and wigs, but these dolls definitely had been played with.

Toys and dolls, in a miniature way, reflect what society was like at the time of their creation. This find couldn't be hurried. It would be time-consuming to look up prices now. I decided to put that off for a while. Toys and especially dolls have become a hot ticket item in today's antique market, and would be exciting for me to evaluate. I thought one might possibly be a Mary Todd Lincoln. If it was I knew it could be worth around a thousand dollars.

Taking a total of ten dolls out of the cardboard box, where they'd slumbered for years, I carefully removed each doll. I placed them gently, one by one, on top of some old newspapers on the attic floor. Several layers of crumpled, yellowed newspapers remained. As I removed the papers, a Victorian dollhouse that looked like the Carter House in miniature popped into view. Its furnishings were still intact. *Ka-ching, Ka-ching* went the cash register in my head. I put everything back in the box and slid it over to the auction side of the room.

I had also found tucked in one corner of that box, a tattered brown envelope. Inside it were several paper dolls from the 1860s. These had been mass-produced by a popular company back then called the McLaughlin

Brothers. All of these paper dolls had removable outfits. By their bedraggled look, they literally had been loved to pieces as they charmed some Victorian child's heart.

Working for a while I didn't unearth anything else exciting and had almost finished for the day. I went down to the second floor to freshen up but when I passed Polly's room I couldn't resist the urge to go in and poke around among her things.

The three wooden armoires, aligned along one wall, looked like they were on a showroom floor and captured my interest. I eased open the door on the one next to the picture window. It was crowded with turn-of-the-century clothes that must have hung on their padded hangers for many years, judging by the amount of accumulated dust that was visible. Another lucrative find! Not true antiques but highly collectible. Vintage clothing was at an all-time premium. Several pairs of high button shoes lay in an untidy heap on a shelf underneath the dresses. I picked up one and dropped it immediately when a centipede crawled out. The shoe hit the bottom of the armoire and made a hollow sound. Stepping back I looked at its dimensions. The piece had to have a false bottom. More than likely there was a cubbyhole that afforded the owner a hiding place for valuables.

Taking all of the shoes from the wooden bottom of the piece I set them on the floor. I began running my hands over the top of the wooden shelf, hoping the creepy crawly centipede had no family members living in there.

My fingers found what they'd been searching for, a small curved indentation. I stuck the end of my index finger in it and wiggled it around. I heard a click.

The bottom of the shelf lifted easily. Maybe the diamond necklace was hidden in here. I was disappointed when I saw the cavity held a clutter of books. If they'd been here for a long period of time I wondered why no dust had collected on them. Had someone been reading these recently? Probably! I opened the top book to the flyleaf and thought it looked like someone's journal. By the dates written in one book I figured that in all probability Polly's mother had written that diary.

I had no clue as to who would be interested in reading these journals except Joe because he'd told me that he was the only one left of the Carter family. Finished working for the day I put the journals in an empty box and carried it to the carriage house. The next time I saw Joe I'd need to ask him what he wanted done with these journals. I would try to remember to tell him about the Mustang in the garage and the value of what I thought it was worth. He probably already knew, but maybe not.

When I reached the apartment I debated with myself whether to go back to Peoria tonight for the weekend or wait until morning. I was dog-tired. Morning won. I investigated what the kitchen cupboards held and came up with one of my old standbys, boiled macaroni, drained with a can of tomatoes added, heavy on the salt and pepper. Not a very well balanced meal, but a personal favorite of mine.

After I ate, I sat down at the desk and flipped on the TV with the remote. Nothing but garbage on the boob tube, so I clicked the set off.

I decided to thumb through the journals that I'd found in the armoire.

17

SHOWERED AND SHAMPOOED, I donned my hot pink flannel robe and fuzzy-wuzzy bunny slippers. I took the journals out of the box, stacked them on the table for a count of twenty-five. Several of them had different faded colors on their covers. Six of the journals were about 8" x 10" with "Diary" embossed slantwise on the cover. Some were not three-ring binders, though of the same size. Four were from the earliest years, and about 5" x 6". I organized them by the different sizes.

I picked up one of the smaller ones at random. Years and deterioration had faded its flowered cover to an unappealing gray-pink. As I flipped through the book a faded sepia snapshot of a curly-headed blonde child sitting on a small wooden rocking chair fell to the floor at my feet. I picked it up and wondered if this could possibly be a picture of Polly when she was a child. There were no particulars written on the back. The child looked to be about two years old and wore a dress. Years ago when this picture must have been taken parents dressed girls and boys alike in little frilly dresses. I couldn't tell what gender the child was but I recognized that little chair. I'd uncovered it from under the decoys in the attic.

When I thumbed through the diaries I could see that they had been written in a random fashion. Large chunks of time were absent. I assumed whoever wrote these diaries must have lost interest, regained it, then begun again. Some of the books were meticulously kept on a daily basis. I organized the volumes by years.

Pouring myself a glass of white wine, I carried it and the earliest book to the couch. Kicking off my slippers I tucked my feet under me and began to read. I quickly realized by the dates that Polly's mother, Sarah Carter, wrote them. The words told about her newly married life and her concerns about moving into the Carter house. Reading it held my interest for a long time but I got too heavy-eyed to read further. My body required sleep.

If I wanted to rise and shine early in the morning for the drive to Peoria I needed to go to bed. I stood up and stretched the kinks out of my back, then reached down and clicked off the lamp. Damn it, I hadn't turned on the light in the bedroom to see by. It was as dark as the inside of a closet at midnight.

Letting my toes search for obstacles on the floor, I inched my way toward the bedroom. When I came even with the picture window I thought I caught a glimpse of a small wavering light in my peripheral vision. I stopped, turned toward the light and was looking into the main house through Polly's bedroom window. I *did* see a light.

There it was again. It moved slowly from side to side. Then bobbed up and down. Someone must be walking around over there with a small flashlight. I wondered why, whoever it was, hadn't turned on the overhead light. Going back to the couch I fumbled around for the phone and took it with me to the window. That little light was still bobbing around in the main house. Should I call 911? I sure as hell didn't want to go over there by myself to find out who it was. It might be a robbery in progress.

I dialed Joe. No answer! I dialed 911. A dispatcher responded, and asked what my problem was. When I explained what was happening, she told me to stay put and she'd send a unit over. I squashed my face up against the window glass trying to see who it could be. The bobbing light went off. A couple of minutes later I heard the crunching sounds of someone running on gravel. The sound grew fainter as they hurried away from the house.

Watching through the window for the police car to arrive I concentrated on breathing slowly in and out, in and out.

Thirty-five minutes went by like molasses dribbling out of a clogged-up jug. I was doing a slow burn and about to call 911 again when a black-and-white with a blinking red cherry on its roof came roaring up the drive. It was a good thing this hadn't been a life or death emergency. I'd passed the Carterville police station on my way to Polly's funeral and knew it was located only five minutes from here.

I watched through the window as the driver yanked the squad car around in a uey. He faced it in the direction from which he'd arrived and slammed on the brakes. The car fish-tailed, peppering loose gravel against the side of the garage. An officer bolted out of the car. He ran around the building and thundered up the stairs.

By that time I was reaching for the doorknob and the light switch, but wasn't quick enough. I flipped on the outside light just as his foot stomped on my non-electric burglar alarm I'd placed in front of the door. Pow, pow, pow, repeated, announcing the mans arrival. I jerked open the door. The outside light I'd turned on spotlighted him where he squatted in one corner of the landing, his gun aimed down the stairs.

"They ran away, officer," I said, and almost giggled because he looked so comical crouching there, caught by my unsophisticated burglar alarm. He looked royally pissed off.

"What the hell was that noise?" he yelped in a high pitched voice. "I think someone just shot at me."

I pointed to the rag rug and flipped up a corner of it so he could see the one-inch bubble wrap his feet had flattened. By the look on his baby face I could tell he wasn't impressed with my inventiveness. By his pale color I suspected he'd been scared spitless.

After I waved him into the apartment, he flashed his credentials "I'm Officer Kidd. What's your name? Spell it for me."

"Annie McMuffit. M C M U F F I T."

"What are you doing in Joe Carter's apartment, Ms. McMuffit?"

"Joe Carter hired me to inventory the antiques in the Carter house. He's allowing me to stay here until I finish the job."

"Why did you call 911?"

"I saw a light over in the main house when I looked through the window here. The light bobbed around in the room that Polly had used. I didn't know but what it might be a break-in to rob the place."

He jotted down the information I gave him in a small spiral notebook he took from his hip pocket "Is that your green Ford Taurus parked in front of the garage?"

"Yes. Why?"

"Ms. McMuffit, it appears as if someone has flattened your tires. Let's go down and take a look for other damage before I check the house."

"Oh my God! I'll get dressed. Be down in a minute,"

I pulled on jeans and a T-shirt, grabbed my jacket, keys, and locked the door behind me. I shoved my burglar alarm rug with my foot to the side so I wouldn't trigger what was left of the bubble wrap when I returned. I hurried down the outside stairs.

My car sat way too close to the ground. If it had legs it would look like a huge green metal elephant kneeling in the gravel. Someone had slashed all my tires. I wasn't frightened now. I was mad as hell. I stomped around my car cussing a blue streak. Goddamnednogoodsonsabitches! Who in the hell did this?" I shouted.

"Do you have any enemies in town, Ms. McMuffit?"

"No one I know of. I've only been here a short time. Why?"

"If you don't have any enemies in town, it is probably vandalism. I'll go over to the main house and see if any damage has been done there."

"You're not leaving me out here alone."

I jogged after him but took one last sad look at my car. Some more of my father, Muley's, Missouri cuss words zipped around in my brain trying to explode from my mouth. We reached the back stairs to the main house.

On the way over I'd been thinking about dealing with that nosey Ron at the service station tomorrow to get four new tires. "Damn! Damn! Damn it. Sonavabitchin' creep." The meaty swear words blasted out of my mouth like a runaway Peterbilt on a steep grade. Officer Kidd looked sideways at me. I could swear he wore a smirk.

When we got to the house I handed the officer my keys. We entered through the back door. The light switches were still the old push-button style that had been popular years ago. I tried to remember where they were.

The downstairs rooms looked undisturbed. We went up the front staircase to the second floor and into Polly's bedroom where I'd seen that flickering light. The shadows disappeared as I pushed the button for the overhead light fixture. My initial observation was that that nothing had been disturbed since I'd left here this afternoon.

"Stay put! I'll inspect the rest of the place."

I was more than willing to stay behind. After he left the room I noticed one of the doors on the armoire that I'd looked through earlier that day, and had taken the diaries from, was half-open. I knew I'd shut it firmly after I put the shoes back inside. I'd heard it click. I reached, using one finger, and slowly inched it open. All that was inside were the same dresses and shoes I'd seen earlier, but the shoes were now lying on one side of the shelf. I'd lined them up neatly.

"Looks like there's no problems here. Let's go," Officer Kidd said as he came back in the room. "Whoever was here must have a key. There's no sign of any break-in."

He locked up the house, handed me my keys then escorted me to the apartment.

The temperature had taken an early, for this time of year dip, and I could see white puffs of vapor our warm breaths generated as we spoke. The officer told me, that he planned to personally let Joe know what happened here. He told me to "rest easy" because he intended to patrol the area frequently throughout the night.

He cautioned me to "stay inside," and stood at the bottom of the stairs until I went into the apartment, closed, and locked the door.

18

JOE KNOCKED ON MY DOOR at seven a.m. I hadn't fallen asleep till after four o'clock. I spent the night turning over and over in my mind what took place here last night. A quick glance in the bathroom mirror reflected my bleary eyes and bed head. That attractive one where the hair flattens on the sides of your head, then comes to a point on top. Like a cone head with hair.

I opened the door and waved Joe in. He took a quick look at the top of my head, then another at my untied tennis shoes peeking out from under my fuzzy robe. The one I wore often that made me look like a giant pink marshmallow. He gave me the once over men of all ages will use when you're not looking your best. I silently blessed his heart for not laughing out loud.

Joe said he came early to wait for Ron to replace the tires on my car. He planned to hang around outside while watching for him.

"I'm going to pay for your new tires, Annie." He bent down and pulled up a corner of the rug where the deflated bubble wrap lay. Joe couldn't contain a grin. I assumed

Officer Kidd had spread the word about my homemade burglar alarm.

I looked Joe in the face, squinted, planted my fists on my hips, and asked, "Is there something you find amusing?"

He cleared his throat noisily. "No, Annie. Just thinking about a joke I heard," he lied. "How you doing after that fright last night?"

"I'm all right now but I was scared silly then. Officer Kidd said he didn't know who it was in the house. How many people have a key, Joe?"

"Me, you, and Mrs. B. She keeps a spare hidden on the ledge above the front door. There's another one under that concrete block by the back porch. I checked, they're both still there. If it was Mrs. B she'd have turned on the lights."

"Did the police talk to her?"

"Yup! Said it wasn't her over here creeping around. And that she hadn't heard anything unusual. Cops told me they would keep an eye out. Said it's probably a kid prank."

"Didn't feel like a prank to me," I grumbled. "Do you know anyone who wouldn't want me here? Maybe whoever it was is trying to run me off."

"Can't think of anyone who would do that. Or why! Probably it's just what Kidd said it was. A prank by some youngster in the neighborhood."

He hadn't convinced me. I still felt like some unknown person didn't want me to be here. I thought about it being Ron. He would make a lot of money from selling four new tires and a service call. I thanked Joe for his help as a truck from the gas station pulled into the drive. Ron soon had four new Michelins on my car. A lot more rubber than my car has worn since I'd bought it second hand.

* * *

Clouds had swallowed the sun. The darkening sky was threatening nasty weather. It was colder than a well-diggers ass in January when I finally got underway to Peoria. I'd called Venus earlier that morning to tell her about the trouble with my car, and that I'd be late getting there today.

I'd been missing my cat Sugar, so thought I would stop by home first and pay her a visit before going to the shop.

Myrtle, my nosy neighbor, was on duty. *Did she never sleep?* It was a certainty that she had the street and the people that live on it under surveillance. Curtains can't move away from a window without help. I should have been delighted that she watched the comings and goings at my house free of charge but it irked me nonetheless.

When I let myself in the back door of my house, I called, "Here kitty, kitty." No kitty appeared. The house felt vacant. Sugar's water and food bowls sat in their proper place next to the refrigerator. They were both empty. I looked everywhere in the house that the cat liked to conceal herself and called her name. No Sugar ran out from any of her favorite hidey-holes. I hoped Venus hadn't let her slip outside.

I got back in the Taurus, drove to the shop and parked on the street in front of Annie's Attic. I always park on the street whenever I can as I think it will appear that a customer is inside. As I walked past the front display window I saw Sugar curled up on a red blanket surrounded by antique toys. Her head lay rotated with her nose pointing to the sky. She usually lay in that position prior to a rain. Maybe she could predict snow, too. Clever cat! I flicked the window with a finger. Sugar slowly uncurled her body and blinked her big blue eyes at me through the glass. By the time I reached the door and opened it, she was there to greet me. I picked her up and stroked her. She rumbled her pleasure.

Venus came out of the back office grinning at me from ear to ear. "Hello, Annie, I wanted to surprise you, so I brought Sugar to the shop with me. She likes it here. I brought her earlier this week, too, and several new walk-by customers saw her in the window and came in just to pet her. She generated two sales and caught a mouse that she spit out at my feet like she was giving me a present."

Venus must have gone to the beauty shop again this week because she was in one of her mahogany colored hair days. She had on a black spandex mini-skirt with a bright, tight orange blouse and white high-top tennis shoes. Orange and black had been my school colors when I went to Manual High School here in Peoria years ago. She looked as if she were about to fire off a "Rah, rah, rah, Sis boom bah" cheer.

Was it my imagination or had her not very sophisticated choices in wearing apparel taken a mighty dip for the worse?

Venus was way past her sell-date.

19

TOMORROW IS MONDAY, another workday. Local TV forecasters had been gloom-and-doom. They warned of approaching rain changing to sleet later in the day. To miss it, I drove back to Carterville on Sunday night. The sky looked sinister and would most likely fulfill the predictions within a few short hours.

Pulling into the drive at the carriage house I hustled up the stairs to the apartment. The gusting wind peppered me with debris and howled in the treetops. I'd found my burglar bubble-wrap contrivance at the foot of the stairs where it had blown. I rolled it up and carried it and my dinner up to the apartment, hurried inside and cranked up the thermostat.

I'd gone over the Murray Baker Bridge into East Peoria to number one on my pizza-eating list, Davis Brothers and brought back my favorite. I sniffed it and drooled all the way here. After popping a couple of slices in the microwave, I opened a can of Pepsi. I sipped and ate while standing in the kitchenette munching my extra crispy sausage, green pepper, onion and triple-cheese pizza.

After a shower I put on my Mickey Mouse T-shirt, robe and slippers then picked up one of the diaries. As I walked to the couch I passed the picture window and could see no scary lights at the main house tonight.

The rain and sleet predicted earlier had started with a vengeance. I like the cozy feeling of being safe indoors when rain pelts the windows and roof. It makes me doubly appreciative of the warmth inside.

I sank down onto the couch to read more about Sarah's life.

The last few pages in the journal seemed to be about her plans for a visit from Polly's fiancé, Harry Cody. Sarah describes the vehicle that Harry drove as "a bootlegger's truck." I wondered if it could be the truck that I'd seen down below in the garage. Nah! I dismissed that thought as unlikely after so many years had passed. I looked for the diary that would continue the saga of Sarah but couldn't find it. Maybe it was still over at the house. I was determined to find it.

Reading the words written in the journals, I felt as though I stood in Sarah's shoes. I'd become a paper voyeur into her life and fancied I could hear her speak the words. After a short while I had trouble keeping my eyes open so called it a night, but felt like I was leaving a good play during intermission.

The next morning for a change of pace, I decided to work in Polly's room. After about an hour I heard the sounds of a hammer on wood, coming from the hallway and poked my head around the door. A man was repairing the wobbly stair railing.

He was short, fat in the middle, and poor on both ends. Untamed white eyebrows grew wild above watery, faded eyes. His chin looked like he'd shaved it with the backside of a razor.

As I approached the man, he said, "I'm here to fix what you need fixin,' little lady." He gave his head a short bob and removed a red Chicago Cubs' baseball cap. His bare head looked like a full moon on the rise. This had to be Mrs. B's husband, Willie, whose shadow, she'd told me, would arrive ten minutes behind him.

I approached him and stuck out my hand. "I'm Annie McMuffit."

He seemed to have a problem with what to do with the hammer, but finally bent over and placed it gently on the floor. He took my hand and shook it limply, once up, then once down.

"Mr. B here! I have a list of chores from the Mrs. I'll do them quick as ever I can."

I assured him that he could take all the time he wanted. By the pleased look that took the place of the anxious one on his face, I assumed he was happy to know that he wouldn't have to hurry.

"Continue," I said flipping him a backhanded wave and returned to Polly's room. I removed two signed Turner oil paintings from the walls, wrapped them in bubble wrap and leaned them by the door for the auction. I began working on the contents of Polly's dresser drawers. I kept my eyes peeled for that vanished diary and the missing diamond necklace.

Later I heard Joe out in the hall asking Mr. B how he was getting on. They had a quiet conversation that I couldn't hear. Joe entered the room where I was working. He was cheerful on this sunless Monday morning.

"Morning, Annie. Got a giant favor to ask of you."

"Ask away Joe."

"Got a serious Sparky problem. Tried all week to find someone to look after him. Have to go to Arizona. Looking at some property there. Gonna retire in Sun City when this mess about Aunt Polly is cleared up. Could you please take care of Sparky for me? He really likes you."

I pondered the request then came to the conclusion that I'd feel safer with Sparky in the apartment. Good old Sparky would bark and warn me if any one came around. "Sure, I'll do it, Joe. I think I'd like having Sparky for company. Bring him over before you leave."

Joe cleared his throat, shuffled his feet. "I've got him in the car now. Time ran out on me. I'm on my way to the airport. Got Sparky's food and water dishes in the car. He likes to go for a long walk every day. Keep him on a short leash though or he'll go off hunting by himself. On this fenced-in property he'll do all right without it. But he's not used to the city. I'd hate for him to get lost here in town."

He must have been pretty sure that I wouldn't turn him down. I followed him to his car that was parked at the curb and tugged Sparky out through the open window. I carried the dog upright, tucked next to me like he was a baby. He gifted me with stinky breath and a face licking. Joe carried the box of doggie supplies, set them on the porch, then took the dog from me. He talked nonsense to it, like I did to Sugar when I had to leave her. Joe deposited the dog back in my arms, gave a wave and with "See you both in a week" spun his wheels.

That night, after the dog and I both took a nap. I was reading in one of the diaries. Sparky had draped himself across my feet. After a short while the dog growled and jumped up. He ran to the door that connected the apartment to the garage. He was barking at full volume, and scratching and snuffling at the crack under it. Someone or something had to be down there. With trembling fingers I dialed 911 again.

By the time Officer Kidd arrived this time whatever or whoever it was had long gone. He went outside and walked around both buildings. He came back and reported, "Ms. McMuffit, most likely it was an animal that set the dog off. Him being a hunting dog, he probably wanted to go out and run it down." What could I do? It seemed like a plausible explanation. I still felt as if someone was trying to frighten me away from here. I wondered why they would do that and who it could be? What had I done to them? What was going on here? Stubborn me, I determined that as long as they didn't kill me I'd continue with what I was doing—and watch closely the people I dealt with here in Carterville.

* * *

Everything went smoothly with Sparky on Tuesday. On Wednesday night I called 911 again when I saw a shadowy silhouette in Polly's bedroom window. It looked to me as if someone was watching me through the window.

A different man drove up in answer to my distress call this time. He introduced himself as Chief of Police Sean O'Reilly. He looked like he'd missed a large number of meals. He was rail thin with noassatall. Freckled pasty skin poked out from under his three-inches-too-short sleeves on his navy blue jacket. His looks matched his voice, reedy and feeble. He had protruding eyes and blinked repeatedly. A serious comb-over started at the top of his right ear. Images of Barney Fife from Mayberry, the popular old television show, came to mind. Sparky sat patiently at my feet and looked up at him.

Every so often, disrupting what he was saying, his face scrunched up in what must be a compulsory habit. It made him look like he was chewing on a hornet.

I explained that I'd seen a silhouette of an unknown person standing in the window of the Carter house, watching me over here. He wrote the information in a small spiral notebook, then returned it to his back pocket. From the annoyed look on his face I got the impression he thought I wanted him to slay an imaginary dragon.

He left after telling me to call the regular number if I had something else to report. That really steamed me. He said the town had a small police force and my 911 calls interfered with their work. I had probably interrupted their hot pursuit of finding a place to catnap, or maybe I'd interrupted them hunting down the town's notorious weenie wagger. The chief definitely was blowing me off.

His instructions were for me to stay indoors at night. Well, duh! I knew what I knew and whoever had been over in the Carter house had been watching me. Why?

I walked to the window without looking across the way, and yanked the drapes closed. I wouldn't open them again until I got to the bottom of who was spooking me and why the odd behavior.

20

SPARKY BARKED AND DARTED up off my feet, and began running in circles in his awkward three-legged gait. He looked like he was chasing his tail. The dog went to the door and looked up at the doorknob. A knock sounded, and I heard Joe say, "It's me, Annie." He had returned earlier than planned.

Joe's voice sent Sparky into a renewed frenzy of running in circles and barking. "Settle down," I told the dog. I took hold of his collar and tugged him away from the door so I could open it.

Man and dog were a sight to behold. I couldn't tell which was happiest. Joe went down on one knee and Sparky hurled his doggie body at him. Joe caught the dog up into his arms and hugged him. "I'm glad to see you too, old fella'." Joe looked sheepishly at me, then put the dog down on the floor. Wriggling Sparky's ears back and forth he asked, "Did he behave himself?"

"He sure did, Joe. He took me for a walk every day. When I let him loose to run on the property he started bringing me things from his forays in the woods like he does you. He hasn't been any trouble at all. I enjoyed his company. As a matter of fact, he came in very handy because I had another scare the night you left."

"What happened?"

I aimed my index finger at the access door to the garage. "Sparky ran over there. He was barking and scratching at the bottom of it. I knew someone had to be down there."

"What'd you do?"

"I called the police again. By the time Officer Kidd arrived, whatever or whoever it was had long gone. He told me he thought it was an animal and that Sparky, being a hunting dog, probably wanted to go out and run it down.

"That wasn't the end of it though. I had to call the police again Wednesday night. I saw a shadow in Polly's window. The Chief of Police came that time. I think they don't believe me. The only advice O'Reilly gave me was 'stay indoors at night.' Whoever was over there in your house was looking in here watching me. I pulled the drapes closed and haven't opened them since. I feel like a prisoner."

"This is a pretty quiet town. Police calls are scarce as curlers on a pig. I'll go by the station and take care of it," Joe promised.

I smiled and thanked him. "Well, anyway, I could at least say, 'Welcome home.' How was your trip? You're back early."

"Trip was about as productive as chasing the wind. Never did like traveling by myself. Decided to come back early."

"Did you find any property you liked, Joe?"

"I found several beautiful houses. Got doubts now though about retiring in Arizona."

"Why is that?"

"For starters it was hotter n' hell there. Here it is November but the temperature there was in triple digits every day. All the natives go around bragging about their damned dry heat. It's dry and hot there, all right. Thought the elastic in my shorts would melt."

"When my father Muley retired to Arizona he'd just turned sixty and said he rather liked the idea of being called a sexagenarian. He said that word sounded sort of flattering to him. I visited his retirement community one time and I couldn't believe the beauty of Arizona—or the changes I observed in Dad."

"It's beautiful, all right. After you wipe the sweat from your eyes so you can see it. What changes did you notice about your father, Annie?"

"The first thing was his dark tan. He said he played golf every day and cards every night with 'the boys.' He also told me that he worked on his sense of humor every time he looked in a mirror at his aging face. Muley developed a five-minute stand up comedy routine and performed it whenever the park management asked him to. His subject matter was—what else? Senior citizens."

"What was his routine?"

"Well, his shtick was a back and forth argument he was having with a woman hidden backstage and playing the role of his wife. His part was a senior gentleman annoyed with his wife. The make-believe wife's strident voice came periodically from backstage warning him over and over not to fall asleep outdoors. She'd tell him about the sun being much hotter in Arizona than it was back in Illinois. He'd bellow his answer 'I never fall asleep outside.' The next time Muley, as the old guy, nodded off in his chair, the pretend wife backstage would say, 'Sleep, you old fool'."

Joe chuckled.

I continued my story. "Onstage, Muley made believe he was in his backyard lounging in a beat-up reclining lawn chair he used as a prop. He tipped his head back, his mouth wide open and made loud snoring noises. With each exhale, his tongue would inch out, little by little, till it reached his chin. Bottom line of his skit was that he had to go to the local emergency room to have his sunburned tongue treated, the 'wife' hauling him over the coals all the way."

Joe laughed loud, long, and hard, during the story's progress and wiped his eyes as I concluded. After he finally quit laughing, he said, "Annie, you're quite a storyteller. I needed that laugh. What did you think of Arizona when you were there?"

"I loved it, Joe. I went in April. It was pretty warm."

"It would take some getting used to for me. Oh, I almost forgot. Mrs. B invited me to dinner tonight at six. Said to ask if you would come over too?"

"Sure, I'll go. I always look forward to eating someone else's cooking."

"I'll take Sparky off your hands now."

I patted the top of the dog's head, and told Joe anytime he wanted to drop him off for a visit to feel free to do so. Happy in their togetherness, man and dog trotted down the stairs. I watched as they got into the Cadillac. Joe lowered his window on the driver's side and Sparky stuck his head out. As they drove away I could see the dog's black nose twitching and his ears flying in the wind.

After they left, I recalled my visit to father in Arizona. I remembered thinking at that time how much I'd like to retire there someday in my murky future. I'd added Arizona to the top of my list that grew longer every year of possible places where I could retire. I was fed up with the Midwest humidity.

The harsh environment I expected to see in Arizona hadn't been realistic. I'd often pictured the desert as it appeared in those movies about the Sahara. Complete with camels, the Foreign Legion, and people crawling in search of water over hot burning sand.

I fell in love with the Arizona desert I saw on that trip, especially the majestic purple mountains pushing up out of the sand. In the mornings for breakfast I went outdoors to father's rock and cactus yard, and picked big juicy oranges off his trees. I ate them letting the juice flow over my chin. The large, flamboyant purple, yellow, or red flowers of the many different varieties of blooming cacti were spectacular. The desert comes alive at that time of the year. Some of the giant saguaros can reach way over fifty feet. They wore their blooms as a halo wreathing the uppermost part of the plant. Many looked like they were in a hold-up with their arms raised in surrender.

Hummingbirds by the dozen came to feed at the bright red sugar water containers that father hung outside his kitchen window. Their showy iridescent feathers flashed in the sun. Quail families, their topknots shaped like commas would run freely in an odd-looking, stop and start single file. Cars braked on the road to let them cross.

I often pictured myself lying in a hammock under clear blue skies sipping on a bottle of Corona beer that had a hint of fresh tangy lime squeezed in it.

On my one visit to Arizona I became a wannabe native. Someday! Someday!

21

I ARGUED WITH MYSELF as I dressed, trying to justify wearing my red stilettos. "Joe likes them" finally won. I put on a black silk sheath with big red roses on it. My clothes, except for the jeans and T-shirts I wore daily, were way over the top for this area. What the hell did I care. I'd never see these people again after I left here. My 'consultant' at the Once Again consignment shop had assured me that I looked elegant in this outfit. My down jacket didn't do much for the ensemble but was the only warm coat I'd brought with me.

Wobbling in my heels down the gravel drive, I left for the B's house. Mrs. B must have heard me approaching, because she met me at the door and ushered me into their 1950s house. It looked as if the dwelling consisted of four small rooms. It was box-like and painted a Caterpillar yellow with green shutters. I winced whenever I looked at it. That shade of yellow is not one of my favorites.

Joe and Willie sat at a card table in the living room and said, "Hello, Annie," in unison.

It looked as though I'd interrupted a game between the three of them. Several cards lay face down, in a fan shape on the table in front of where Mrs. B sat down.

She pointed at the vacant chair and said, "Sit, Annie." I sat.

"Wait till we finish this three-handed pinochle game, then we'll talk," Joe said, continuing to play cards. Three unsmiling faces watched their opponent's expressions for a reaction to any given card they chose from those in their hand. They slapped the card down in the middle of the table. Whoever prevailed took what I soon learned was called a trick. Then they each took the cards lying in front of them and counted in a puzzling, to me, method. Joe tallied the scores after they finished playing and declared himself the winner. Couldn't prove it by me. I didn't know how to play pinochle.

"Do you play any card games, Annie?" Willie asked.

"I only know how to play solitaire."

"What say we teach you a new game after we eat? The Mrs. and I learned one called Hand and Foot last month? Do you want to try it?"

"Card games never played a big part in our family entertainment, but I'm willing to try, if it's not too complicated."

"Makes you put your thinking cap on," Joe grinned, and winked at me.

When I heard Mrs. B puttering around in the kitchen, I went in and asked if I could help prepare dinner.

"Everything's under control in here, Annie. Go set a spell in the living room. Dinner should be ready in about ten minutes."

As I left the room I caught sight of two empty boxes of fast-to fix-macaroni and cheese, plus a mound of potato and onion peelings in the garbage can. That observation and the smell of fried onions gave me an inkling of the menu tonight. Ohhhh, yeah, yummy, yummy carbohydrates for my thighs and tummy as I recollected Mrs. B's lack of culinary skills.

Joe and Willie had their heads bent close to one another, deep in a discussion when I returned to the living room. Not wanting to disturb them, I wandered around the room then browsed the contents of a fake oak, do-it-your-self bookcase that looked like a blue-light special from Kmart, and most likely assembled by Willie. I was reading the spines on the books lined up on the shelves when my eyes locked onto a small volume lying flat on the bottom shelf, half covered by a *Reader's Digest*. I nudged the *Digest* away from the book with the toe of my shoe and saw "Diary" embossed on the front cover. It was identical to those other books I'd found hidden in Polly's armoire. I just knew this had to be that missing diary I'd been searching for. I wanted to continue the saga of Sarah. I wanted that journal. *Down girl, play it cool.*

Mrs. B, just possibly, might be the person I'd seen prowling around inside the Carter house and outside by the garage on the night Sparky raised such a ruckus. Or was it Mr. B? Probably not, but I wasn't ruling him out.

My fingers twitched from wanting to simply pick the book up and deposit it in the bottom of my purse. I couldn't see any way to sneak it. My pocketbook was on the bed with my jacket. At least I now knew where the book was and could quit looking for it. I had a hunch the answers to Joe's family questions would be written in its pages.

I didn't want to ask Mrs. B why she had the book because she'd already denied being in the house with a flashlight. My gut feeling was that she probably had been in the process of taking the rest of the diaries away with her, but I took them before she could. I didn't know why she wanted them. She was only Polly's caregiver, wasn't she?

Words buzzed in my head. A plan! A plan! I need a plan.

Mrs. B called out in her usual "Yoo hoo" fashion signaling us to come to the table. I turned toward Joe and Willie. Joe took my elbow and escorted me into the dining area, which was a corner of the kitchen. A large bowl of macaroni and cheese sat in the middle of the table and next to it was a platter mounded high with a burnt offering of fried potatoes and onions. The lunches I'd eaten since I took this job hadn't improved since the first day so I shouldn't have been surprised at this odd repast.

Joe and Willie sat at the table and dug in, after piling huge amounts of food on their plates. They passed the bowls to me and I took small helpings, then passed them on to Mrs. B. I tried desperately for some kind of a positive to give her, so finally told her that I appreciated them sharing their dinner with me tonight. She smiled and nodded acknowledgment.

It didn't take long for the men to wolf down their food. Then both picked up their spoons and looked expectantly at Mrs. B. She chuckled. "You men never get tired of my blackberry cobbler do you?"

Juicy blackberries had been turned into a mouth-watering cobbler hot out of the oven and proudly carried to the table by Mrs. B. We each had two helpings of the hot, luscious cobbler smothered with heavy cream. I had a real positive to give this time and said, "I think I've died and gone to heaven. That cobbler was delicious. Best I've ever eaten. May I have the recipe?"

Mrs. B smiled. "Sure thing, Annie."

Joe drove me back to the carriage house. I was infinitely grateful that I didn't have to walk back over the gravel in high heels. We'd left about nine o'clock after the three of them gave me a lesson in how to play the card game Hand and Foot. It was relatively simple and fun, but time-consuming.

Before I got out of his car, Joe asked if I'd like to go with him to one of his favorite eating places in Canton next week, on Friday night.

"I'd love to go with you, Joe. It sounds like a nice break in my work routine."

Joe smiled as his assessing eyes traveled over me. "Wear what you have on Annie, I really like it."

Thinking ahead to tomorrow, Saturday morning, I planned my trip to Peoria. I intended to ask Venus to be my sounding board while I mulled over what to do next. I needed to develop a plan for how I could pilfer the diary from Mrs. B's house. I thought it mighty strange that she had possession of it but denied involvement with the strange goings-on at night over in the main house.

I desperately wanted to read what was in that particular diary to satisfy my curiosity. Would I find Carter secrets between its covers? My most important question was why she'd chosen that specific journal to filch over all of the others?

22

WHEN I LET MYSELF INTO THE SHOP I didn't know what came over Sugar. She jumped about four feet in the air, did a flip, landed on all four and zipped in back of the jewelry display case. She looked like a cardboard cutout of that black hump-backed Halloween cat, except she was white. She whipped out from behind the jewelry case and skittered around the room then darted behind the counter by the cash register. I suspected she might smell Sparky's doggy odor on me. She didn't like being in the presence of any dog and acted foolish if that happened. If that were her problem, she would no doubt settle down later and start sucking up to me.

Venus and I discussed on the phone last night my opening the shop for business this Saturday morning. In case there was something she needed to do, I told her to take a half-day off and to come in around noon.

After I started a pot of coffee brewing, I grabbed some rags, a bottle of Windex, the can of paste wax, and began the never-ending job of dusting and glass cleaning that takes place in the shop daily.

The assorted objects in the window display needed dusting more than any place else so I started there. I was never satisfied with how the articles looked after I rearranged them and had intended to devote some time learning the art of merchandising. It seemed I spent my time just trying to keep the business stable.

Standing up, I planted both hands on my hips and bent backwards trying to ease a stitch in my side. When I straightened up I was delighted to see that a very pretty woman somewhere in her late twenties was entering the shop. She clutched the hand of a little girl. The woman had to be the little one's mother as she'd virtually cloned herself in a pocket-sized way. They both wore their thick, long, silvery blonde hair pulled up into ponytails and adorned with a bright red satin ribbon. Their identical almond shaped emerald green eyes roamed around the shop as if they were looking for something specific. I was reminded of Mother and myself when we'd haunted the antique shops so many years ago.

"Good morning, may I help you find something?"

Sugar came out from behind the counter where she'd been sulking and began weaving her body in and out around the little girl's stubby legs.

"Look Mommy, here's that pretty white kitty we saw."

Her mother bent and stroked Sugar's back, kindling audible purring. The woman smiled and stood up and looked down at her daughter who was petting Sugar.

"This cat is what we're looking for. Melissa and I came in last Wednesday after seeing the cat in the window. My daughter fell head over heels in love with it. The pretty white kitty-cat is all she's talked about since then. We came back to visit."

"The cat's name is Sugar," I told them. "It seems she's as love-struck with Melissa as Melissa is with her."

The little girl sat on the floor tucking her legs to make a lap. Sugar crawled into it and licked Melissa's chin.

Fickle damned cat!

I rang up the first sale of the day, a pair of salt and peppers.

It interests me when people buy shakers. I usually ask them if they have a collection. If they do, I ask how many sets they have. Melissa and her mother had a small collection of thirty. With these it would be thirty-one.

A person can take a stroll down memory lane as each set of shakers takes them back to a different era. It's like holding up a mirror to the past.

Before salt became refined, processed, and free-flowing as we know it today, it was necessary to serve it in a container called a salt cellar. That cellar would be placed at the host's location on the dining table. It would be passed from person to person, and a small spoon used to sprinkle salt over the food. In 1858, John Mason invented the screw top saltshaker and collecting them soon became a fashionable trend. Novelty shakers at that time usually dealt with animals, fish, birds, characters, or well-known people. The categories evolved through the years into a vast number of designs.

My mother had a collection of over one hundred. As a child, when standing eye-level with our dining room table, I would gaze at the colorful shakers she'd chosen to use that day.

Happy with their purchase and at finding "the pretty white cat" again, mother and daughter left as Venus came in the door.

"Did you have a good morning?" I asked.

"Yep! Ate an early lunch at the restaurant over on Sterling Avenue. I ran into Oscar there. He's an old friend of mine. Oscar used to run an antique shop in Canton where I lived years ago. He's coming to the shop today. I want to introduce him to you. He rattles off descriptions, prices of antiques, and their history just like you do, Annie."

"There's fresh coffee if you want some, Venus. When you've caught your breath, I'll tell you what's happening in Carterville. I need your valued input about several things."

Venus poured coffee in the purple mug with a picture of Bugs Bunny she'd claimed as hers when she first started working here. We both sat in the office, me at the desk, Venus in the "client" chair.

"Fire away," Venus said as she pointed her index finger at me.

"Do you remember my telling you about that missing diary? The one I've been looking for everywhere?

Venus nodded.

I continued, "And do you remember my telling you that Mrs. B said it wasn't her with the flashlight over in Polly's room the first time I called 911?"

Venus nodded.

"Well, Joe came home early from his trip to Arizona. Mrs. B invited us to their house for dinner last night, and guess what? I spied that diary on the bottom shelf of her bookcase."

"No kidding! Did you get it?"

"Not with Joe and Willie in the same room. I know curiosity killed a cat, but I'm becoming curiouser and curiouser. I want to know what is written in that particular diary that would cause someone to do all of that sneaking around. Makes me wonder if it could have been Mrs. B both times I called 911. Or maybe it was Mr. B. It could have been Ron, from the gas station too. I've seen him over at the B's house a good deal of his off work times.

Can you help me with a plan to get that diary out of the B's house? I won't rest till I read it."

"Sure! Does Mrs. B have a daily routine, Annie?"

"She fixes my lunch Mondays through Fridays at noon so she'd be over at the main house then."

"Is there any other time she's routinely away from home?"

"That's the only occasion I know about."

142

"Is Mr. B at the house all the time? Does he have a daily routine?"

"I don't know. If I want him to fix something he's never been very reliable about when he would do it. Mrs. B says he does everything at the speed of a candle melting. After meeting him I'd have to agree with her."

"What hours does Ron work?"

"Six a.m. till three."

"Sounds like a job for 'Snooper Venus.' Mrs. B will be at the Carter house fixing your lunch at noon. Ron will be at work. I can lure Mr. B out of their house then. You could sneak over and take the diary."

"But you have to be here, remember?"

"We could ask Oscar to cover for me here at the shop while I drive to Carterville for a few hours. Oscar's really a good guy. He's honest. Besides that I'm curious too. I've been wanting to see the people and places you talk about."

"Sounds do-able, Venus, but I have to check out Oscar first. We'll see about it then. He may not even want to work here."

"Well, Annie, when I talked to him this morning he sounded like he was bored out of his gourd. He lives in that high-rise senior retirement building over on Sterling. I think he'd want to do it. He told me he feels like he's the only one living there who can put a sentence together with more than three words in it. And if I remember right

Oscar had a real special way of merchandising in his store. Maybe we could pick up a few pointers."

23

WHEN OSCAR SHULTZ, Venus's friend, entered the shop he looked to be about seventy, and then some. I'm five foot two and he wasn't much taller than I, but looked firm and fit for a gentleman of his obvious years.

He wore his sparse silver-white hair in a short-cropped crew cut over a broad, low hairline. A tangle of white eyebrows grew in an untidy straight line over his clear slate- colored eyes. He had a broad nose, meaty ears, and well-shaped lips with a deep indentation at the right corner of his mouth giving the impression that he wore a continuous lop-sided grin. Crosshatched with wrinkles, Oscar's skin had the rosy tone of a person with high blood pressure. It looked shiny as though polished. He was clean-shaven and the faint unmistakable scent of Old Spice faintly surrounded him.

After Venus introduced us Oscar reached out a slender hand, took mine, and pumped it enthusiastically. "Hello Annie, nice to meet you. Great shop you have here. How's business?"

"Business is extremely slow," I admitted. "But I'm an optimist. Tomorrow it may pick up again. I've been working in a small town on an extensive project. Venus minds the shop while I'm away."

"Is there anything I can do to help out? I've had a lot of experience in a place similar to this one in Canton before I retired. I started it when I quit farming for something to keep me occupied. I found out, after I quit working that I failed retirement 101. I'm not a do-nothing guy, have to keep busy. I've wished many times I hadn't given up my shop."

Venus and I were a captive audience for Oscar, and he was a talker. That can be a good thing in this business but you also need to be able to read people to know when they want to talk, and when they want to browse. It's almost a sixth sense successful vendors seem to have. I'd lay twenty-to-one odds that Oscar was a skilled salesman.

I began picking his brain. I asked about the basics for merchandising he'd used in his shop.

He got right into it. "First I selected the items to go on display. Usually things that were on the inventory sheet too long. I tried to turn over my merchandise monthly. I grouped similar objects together. Positioned small things in front of large ones, a single antique can look very important when displayed by itself topping a mirror. I liked to display items in small groupings according to form, function, medium or color. My favorite display was the one I called 'The Vintage Greens.' On the back wall of my shop I hung a large green and white cotton quilt, then placed everything green I could find in the shop on the shelves directly underneath the quilt. Green Depression glass dishes, kitchen gadgets with green handles, green fiesta-ware. Well, you get the picture.

"I liked to discover new ways to display items using a sense of humor. Do you want me to show you what I would do for a laugh in here?"

"Please do, Oscar." I was captivated by this man's knowledge.

"Okay. See those vintage hats lined up on this shelf?"

I nodded and he continued, "They're taking up valuable space." Oscar walked to a music display I had set up last month and carried a bust of Beethoven to a round oak table displaying a few small items. Dealers called these items 'Smalls' in the antique business. He removed all of the smalls from the table, placing them on a half-empty shelf. Oscar carried an oak cheval floor-length mirror from its place by the front door. Placing it next to the table he proceeded to pile hats on top of Beethoven's head until the stack was about three feet tall.

"Now the customers will be able to try these hats on and see what they look like on their own heads. Maybe they'll have a few belly laughs while they're in here." He plopped a ridiculous looking pink picture hat festooned with pink flowers and feathers on top of his head. "I guarantee you the customers will remember what a fun time they had here in your shop. That could generate a return visit."

Venus and I giggled at how funny Oscar looked as he stood there with his red face peeking out from under the silly wide-brimmed pink hat.

He grinned and took off the hat and put it on top of the pile on Beethoven's head. Oscar pointed to the shelf that was now empty. "Now you have this emptied space available to display different bits and pieces from your stockroom.

Venus wore a wide grin on her face the entire fifteen minutes it took Oscar to enlighten us about how he merchandised. "Didn't I tell you he'd be a gold mine?" she asked.

I pulled Oscar to me and gave him a great big yellow rock hug and thanked him for the information. He knew this business, and did I ever need him. The hug had been my big "yes" and we came to an understanding about his wages right then and there. He agreed to fill in for Venus when she came to Carterville after we'd decided on what day it would be. Maybe I'd ask him later if he and Venus wanted to share work time in the shop.

After Oscar left Annie's Attic, Venus and I decided on what day she was to come to Carterville. I told her to call Oscar and ask him to fill in for her so she could arrive at Carterville this coming Wednesday at 11:45 sharp. Timing was crucial to our plan.

When she arrived, she was to stop at Mr. and Mrs. B's house and pretend she was lost. If our scheme worked smoothly Mrs. B would be in the kitchen at the main house and Mr. B would offer to escort Venus there. I, in the meantime, would be positioned outdoors at the back corner of the house.

When I heard Venus and Mr. B enter the front door I would hightail it to their house, snatch the diary, then hurry back to the Carter place. I'd then dash up the stairs to the attic and conceal the book. When Mrs. B "Yoo-hooed" me to come to the kitchen for lunch, I would stroll, ever so serenely downstairs and act surprised when I saw Venus standing there.

The only scenario I could think of that might make "Operation Diary" unsuccessful was if Venus's timing was off. If she arrived too late or too early that would royally screw up things.

24

ON OPERATION DIARY DAY everything fell into place with the precision of an army drill team. I watched from the front second story window. I saw Venus drive up and park her pink Volkswagen at the curb in front of the B's house. It was 11:45. She was right on schedule. The middle of the stairs emitted squeaks and groans where stepped, so I stealthily, awkwardly traveled downward straddling the center of each step. I probably looked like a cowboy too long in the saddle.

I went out the front door, and hid from view among the dying leaves of a lilac bush and listened for Venus and Mr. B to walk up the driveway to the house. After a short time I heard Venus laughing and talking in a loud voice. She would have made a damned fine actress. A squeaky hinge sound of the front door opening followed by a loud bang, as it slammed shut clued me in where they were.

Venus was following our plan.

Now it was my turn to thicken the plot. I hotfooted down the drive and veered left to Mr. and Mrs. B's house. I crept up the porch stairs and turned the doorknob. The door was unlocked. I pushed it open inch-by-inch. I stuck my head in and whispered, "Hello, is anyone here?"

No answer! Good!

My feet felt like they'd been super-glued to the wooden floor of the porch. If I entered this house I would cross a line into the illegal world of B and E in police jargon.

Why in the hell was I so worried? Where had my backbone gone? After all I was here to work for Joe, wasn't I? If I thought the B's house held a secret that would get to the bottom of this deepening mystery here in Carterville, then so be it. I said "Please, God, save me," but had no salt to pinch like I did when I was a little girl. I was about to become a criminal.

Shoving my inconvenient thoughts to the back of my mind I tiptoed into the B's living room. Treading quietly to the bookcase I held my breath. I stretched my hand out toward the bottom shelf with my fingers open like a lobster's claw. The diary wasn't there. *Crapola*. That hadn't even been on my list of things that could possibly go wrong.

I did a quick search of the other shelves in the bookcase, then scanned the room. I didn't see it anywhere. Damn, Damn, double damn it!

"Think! Think! Think," I told myself, smacking my forehead. If I were Mrs. B where would I stash that diary? Like in a cartoon, a light bulb went on over my head. Of course, she probably had deposited it in "the bottomless pit." Her words for the purple, outsized needlepoint bag she totes with her everywhere. Or maybe Mr. B hid it in his toolbox, or Ron could have it at the gas station.

I was running out of time. I needed to hurry back to the house so Mrs. B could call me downstairs for my surprise. I dashed out the door, and ran back to the Carter house, slipping in as quietly as I could through the front door.

Zipping like a bullet to the attic, my legs straddled the middle of the stairs in order to miss the groans and creaks. I took a few minutes to slow my breathing. When I'm frightened or anxious, and I was both now, I've been known to pass out from hyperventilating. Breathing into a brown paper bag usually relieves the lightheadedness. I didn't have a sack so tried the old trick of counting slowly. With pursed lips I said one, one hundred, two, one hundred, three, one hundred, a breathing technique I'd taught emergency room respiratory patients. That system usually works just as well as the paper bag but it takes a little longer.

I heard Mrs. B call from the bottom of the stairs in her customary "Yoo hoo." My signal to come to the kitchen for lunch. This time she tagged on, "I have a surprise for you today, Annie." With my breathing restored to almost normal I moseyed down the servants' back stairs and entered the kitchen.

Venus was standing next to the table looking more ornamental than useful. She'd chosen to wear an ankle length, hot pink, rayon dress that was the same shade as her car. The dress looked like a size six and hugged her size twelve body intimately. Black high-tops peeked out from under its hem. Chandelier rhinestone earrings brushed her shoulders, twinkling from both ear lobes.

I glanced over at Mr. B. where he leaned against the refrigerator. The look on his face confirmed my long time belief that Venus, even at her advanced age, held a certain appeal for the opposite sex. Women usually just stare at her as Mrs. B was doing now. Older men like Mr. B, after taking one look at her, suck in their stomachs and stretch up as tall as they can get, reaching for a macho look. Mr. B gazed longingly at Venus. His expression was like that of an ant on its way to a picnic.

Venus is definitely not a candidate for a pair of wings.

"Surprise!" said Mrs. B, as she pointed at Venus.

Venus slithered over to where I stood just inside of the doorway. She gave me a hug, but was looking out the corner of her eyes at Mr. B. "Thought I'd surprise you, Annie, so I got in my little car this morning, and here I am." She chattered on, "I passed a real bad accident on Route 24 just before I got to Little America." I wondered if she'd ever seen a real good accident.

Mrs. B announced, "There's lunch enough for everyone," as she opened another can of chicken noodle soup and added it to the pot on the stove. "Sit, sit, sit yourselves down everybody."

We sat. Lunch was over in ten minutes. After we finished Venus thanked Mrs. B, said "Toodles" while wriggling her fingers at Mr. B.

We left the kitchen and put our heads together just outside its door to make a few quick plans. I whispered, "I couldn't get the diary. It wasn't there." That brought forth a raised eyebrow from Venus meaning, "I need more information."

We giggled like two schoolgirls when we overheard Mrs. B tell Willie, "Go on home now you old fool. Imagine making googly eyes at your age!" Clatter-bang went a pan. She went on, "I'm going in to Canton now and put some of *our* money in circulation, so fix your own damned supper. Don't wait up for me." Slam went the kitchen door.

Venus and I left by the front door. I asked if she had any room left in her stomach for some real food.

"Good God, yes. Is soup what you get for lunch every day?"

"Yes, but once in a while Mrs. B makes me a Spam sandwich. We'll get a sub, bring it back to the apartment and eat there."

"Hot damn," Venus, said.

I laughed at her enthusiasm. We beat feet to her car she calls "Pinky." We squeezed in and zoomed to Cartervilles's Sub sandwich shop. I went in and came back out carrying a foot long BMT. Back in the apartment I put on a pot of coffee and quickly showed Venus the place.

She said, "Nice set-up, Annie, lets eat!"

I pulled the drapes open and we sat on either end of the couch with our sandwich halves and coffee.

"I'm so glad I came, Annie. Now I can picture the Carter house, the B's house, the town, and your place here when you talk about them."

"Do you want to look through the Carter house, Venus?"

"I don't have time. I promised Oscar I'd be back by three. He has a visitation to go to. Do you know yet what you're going to do about that missing diary?"

"Damned if I know. I'll probably keep looking."

25

EARLY THURSDAY MORNING I dog-sat Sparky for Joe so he could take care of some paper work at the bank in Carterville. Something to do with liquidating his assets. He told me that he took Sparky into the bank once and the dog made a deposit on the floor right in front of their big vault. Mr. Murphy, the president of the bank, asked Joe not to bring Sparky in the bank again.

The wind had picked up. I threw the components of my non-electric burglar alarm rug contraption inside the apartment door. I was on my way over to the Carter house. At the top of the landing, outside the apartment door, I unclipped Sparky from his leash. He bounded down the stairs. The dog disappeared into the woods, his favorite haunting place, just as Chief O'Reilly turned into the driveway.

He parked his car as I reached the bottom of the stairs and I stopped to see what he wanted. He climbed out of the black-and-white, and shoved his hands in his pants pockets.

"Morning, Chief, what brings you here?"

"Coming to ask you about a question I have, nothing official."

"What's the question?"

"Have you found any guns yet? I'm a collector."

"No. I haven't unearthed any weapons so far. Do you want me to let you know if I do?"

Sparky ran out from in between two large oak trees wagging his tail. He darted over to where we stood talking, sat down in the gravel and looked up into my face. I could see that he'd been digging again by the small amount of dirt piled in an upside down V on the top of his nose. A tiny piece of disintegrating brown cloth dangled from the side of his mouth.

Chief O'Reilly bent down and waggled Sparky's ears. "Whatcha' got there, boy?" Tugging the dog's offering out of his mouth he looked at it for a long time. He stood up and slipped it into his back pocket.

I explained the game the dog liked to play with Joe and that he had now included me in his sport. "When Sparky is off his leash, he'll more often than not bring something like that from the woods. I've never followed him but he can't get off the property because it's all fenced in. He must be finding the things here.

"Chief O'Reilly, I've been wanting to apologize for calling 911 so often in the past. I'm still questioning why someone might try to frighten me away. I haven't been in this town long enough to make enemies. What do you think?"

O'Reilly thought that over for a while, screwed his face around, and said, "I've been thinking that old Ms. Polly didn't just fall from the widow's walk. She had to have some help doing it."

"I've been wondering about that too. So, what I hear you saying is you think Polly was murdered?"

"Well, not exactly! What I'm saying is that I have a lot of questions that bother me."

He ticked off his questions on his fingers. I filed them away in my gray matter to think about later:

Who helped Polly take a nosedive off of the widow's walk?

What was she doing up on the roof?

Why did she go there?

When did her diamond necklace disappear?

Where is that necklace now?

And the last question, how did she get up on the roof when she supposedly never left her bedroom.

O'Reilly did his hornet chewing face. I watched in amazement. When his features relaxed into his *normal* face again, I asked, "Do you have any suspects in mind?"

"I'm taking a wait-and-see approach. So far nothing points to anyone in particular. I have a few persons of interest in mind. Keep all of this information under your hat, Annie. Okay?"

"Trust me. I wouldn't dream of interfering." *Not much anyway.* My detective juices were flowing. "Chief, can you tell me who you think it might be? I could watch them for you. Do you think I'll be safe here?"

"I don't think anyone wants to harm you, Annie. All they seem to want is to scare you away from here. Maybe they think you'll uncover some dirty little secret hiding in that house."

I asked him again who he thought could be spooking me, but he wouldn't give me a name. I'd been turning over in my head the pros and cons of telling Chief O'Reilly about the diaries I found, but decided to keep the information to myself. I'd share it with him when I uncovered who, what, when, where, why, and the how of it. Besides, he'd no doubt want to impound the diaries before I could read them.

I needed this job to keep my business afloat and no 'will o' the wisp' spook, was going to get me to leave. The idea of my becoming a rookie detective appealed to my inquisitive nature. I conjured up, what my new business card might look like:

Annie McMuffit
Confidential Investigations
Call 309-DETECTS

Chief O'Reilly scratched his head, studied the ground. Then asked, "Have you met anyone in Carterville by the name of Berni?"

"No. Why?"

"Listen, I'm only telling you this because I need your eyes and ears here at the house. When the medical examiner turned Ms. Polly's body over after she fell to her death, we could see that her arm had covered some scratched out letters in the dirt. The letters were smudged but the ME and I both thought it looked like Berni." He spelled out the letters, "B..E..R..N..I…" We're watching this place, and have been tailing you for your own protection."

His car radio squawked out a message about a rollover on Route 24. O'Reilly left with our conversation dangling.

I headed in the direction of the Carter house with Sparky at my heels bouncing on his three legs. Up the back stairs we went, me to work on the second floor, Sparky to ease himself under Polly's bed with the dust bunnies, to take a nap. *Oh, for a dog's life!*

At ten o'clock, Joe came by the house to collect his dog and I settled into the now familiar routine of appraising.

26

IT WAS FRIDAY ALREADY. Joe phoned in the early morning to see if I could meet him in Canton for our date to dine out, instead of him coming back here to pick me up. It seems he had a meeting with a new lawyer there concerning selling off his assets. He told me he expected to spend a couple of hours at Brown, Brown & Brown, a father, son, and grandson law practice. I told him, "No problem." He told me to meet him at Mama Mia's restaurant on Main Street around six.

Dates at my age are scarce as lilacs on Christmas morning. Meeting Joe in Canton couldn't exactly be called a date but came close enough to make me happy. I wore my black dress with the big red roses on it and the red stilettos he'd asked me to wear after we'd had dinner at the B's house. I was getting a lot of mileage out of the outfit.

Typical Midwest up-and-down weather for the middle of November became a reality as I began my trip into Canton. By the time I arrived there the monster of a severe freezing rain, sleet, and snow predicted for tonight metamorphosed into a pussycat. The closer I got to Canton the clearer the sky became. The severe weather had run out of bluster.

I parked in Mama Mia's half-full concrete lot and glanced at my watch. I was early so decided to walk down Main Street in the direction of an antique mall, Step Back in Time. I'd seen the place on my last trip into Canton. I could kill half an hour until it was time to meet Joe. I intended to look around inside the place for any bargains to purchase for resale at my shop in Peoria.

As I approached the building I saw Ron and an elderly woman entering the antique mall. She was wearing a Walmart mink that made her look like a short wooly bear from behind. Ron carried a medium-sized cardboard box cradled in his arms, the flaps closed. I wondered what was in it.

Oh boy! I was about to start detective work for the first time. I didn't want them to see me so slunk diagonally across the street from the place and hid in an alcove between two buildings there.

As I observed them going about their business through the plate glass window I felt as if I were looking at a really, really big television set with the sound on mute. Ron took several items out of the box one by one, and placed them on a table. The objects looked like they might be antiques, or at the very least, collectibles. The old woman picked up a rag and proceeded to polish each piece, before placing them on several different levels of shelving. She picked up, dusted, and rearranged all of the items already on those shelves to accommodate the new merchandise.

Hmmmm! Did I remember seeing those dark brown Morton pottery pieces at the Carter house?

The two of them talked with their heads close together, nodding and gesturing. I wondered again who the woman might be. I couldn't remember running into her anywhere in Carterville. She was too old to be Ron's mother. Maybe she was his grandmother.

Then I speculated about the items they were arranging on the shelves and wondered spitefully if Ron had stolen them. He came to the Carter House on Monday, Wednesday, and Friday. I always stack items next to the back door ready for him when he comes to burn junk on those evenings. He wouldn't have to enter the house for any reason but could easily have slipped in and helped himself to whatever he wanted.

I hadn't liked him the first day I came to Carterville after my run-in with him at the gas station. I still didn't like or trust him. He acted sneaky.

The building housing the antique mall was a one-story, red brick sitting in the middle third of the block with similar buildings at either end. The three buildings utilized the inner walls as a shared one, probably to save money when constructed.

This mall was the type where vendors rent cubicles. The renter is obligated to keep his or her own display area dusted, swept, updated and rearranged on a weekly basis.

The usual custom for this type of place is that the owners of the mall will either work full time or hire someone to be there around the clock to receive the money when items were purchased. At the end of each month the owner tallies the renter's sold items and writes a check for that amount, minus their rent for the next month.

I continued to watch while concealed in the shadows as Ron and the old woman exited the mall. They climbed in his gray, work-in-progress, truck and rumbled away. A dirty rag waved from the gas tank cavity where a cap should have been. The lazy man. He worked at a gas station but didn't take very good care of his own vehicle.

The truck looked like a Molotov cocktail on wheels.

27

JOE HAD NOSED HIS CADILLAC into the parking spot next to my Taurus by the time I made it back to the restaurant. Good, he was here. I was hungry.

Noise blasted out the door as I entered Mama Mia's place. An intense bouquet of wine mingled with garlic odor was heady, as if someone sprayed an Italiano scent with a free hand.

When I told the "wait-in-line" person I was meeting Joe Carter, she told me, "He's waiting for you." She looked me up and down over the top of her bifocals and said, "He asked me to watch for a good-looking woman wearing a black dress with big red roses. You've got to be her."

She escorted me to the back room where Joe sat fidgeting with his silverware. He stood up as I arrived, then slid in the booth next to me after I was seated. He turned, smiled and asked, "Are you hungry Annie?"

"Starved!"

"Got a favorite dish you like?"

"I always order Eggplant Parmesan, salad, and garlic breadsticks in an Italian restaurant."

The waitress, who'd been hovering at the empty booth next to us zipped over to take our orders when she saw us put the menus down. Joe took the ordering in hand, lasagna for him, eggplant for me and, of course, a bottle of Italian red.

Dishes rattling and gabbling people were the same here as in my favorite place in Peoria and so noisy it was next to impossible to hold a conversation. I'd complained about the noise once in Peoria and the manager had told me, "I like to think the sound is that of people having fun and not noise." That was a good line he'd used to cover the fact that the acoustics in the place were damned near nonexistent.

Our conversation went smoother with Joe seated next to me. When the waitress brought our bottle of wine he poured for both of us. I tapped his half-full glass against mine and made an Italian toast, "Chin-Chin" which means "to your health."

Last Christmas I'd made the same toast to a Japanese friend of mine. I couldn't understand why he looked at me with such a weird face. He finally told me the word Chin in Japanese means penis. He couldn't understand why I would be toasting his. I thought I'd be safe using it with Joe.

"Been wanting to tell you something, Annie. You're doing a damned fine job at the house."

"Thanks, Joe, so thoughtful of you to say. I dislike putting a damper on this nice evening but I need to talk to you about time and money."

"Talk away."

"I'm not even close to finishing inventorying. I need more work time to get ready for the auction if we're going to have it ready by our target date of the first week in January. In one week it will be the end of our four-week agreement. We need to make another contract.

"Don't have a problem with that, Annie. Matter of fact I wanted to ask you about that very thing." He reached into his back pocket and wrote a check for eight thousand dollars for an additional four weeks of work. I still had four thousand from the last check in the bank. With this one I wouldn't have to worry about past due notices for a very long time.

"I'll get the agreement papers ready for you to sign tomorrow, Joe."

The waitress brought our orders. We talked as we ate.

"Is there an auction house you have in mind that you want me to use?"

"I'm leaving that up to you, Annie."

Passing him a business card, I said, "This is the one I think you should use. They offer a complete service. That includes all of the personnel needed for the sale and the equipment that it takes to set up one. You know, tables and things of that nature. The whole process is pretty time-consuming. From the amount of items to go on display in the house I'd say it might take them a week to get it ready. Joe read the card I'd given him, tapped it on the table, and said, "Looks like AUCTIONS R US will be it."

"The closer we get to the actual sale time, the more excited I get about it. A lot of people will be interested at that season. With cold weather at its peak they'll be trying to think of something to do to beat their winter boredom. An auction inside a nice warm house would be a welcome activity. I even wrote a slogan for the paper. Want to hear it, Joe?"

"Ummm hummm!" Joe sipped his wine.

"Roses are red, violets are blue, gifts of antiques, are better than new." I recited.

"Cute!" Joe said "Just like you."

Oh my God, is he flirting?

I decided to stick with business and had some detective questions I wanted to ask, so jumped right in.

"I'd like to talk about what's going on at the Carter house. Chief O'Reilly came by and asked if there would be any guns in the sale. He told me he's a collector."

"Yeah! I knew that about him. Let him know if you find any. Though I don't think you will."

"Joe, I need to ask if you have any idea of who or why someone seems to be trying to scare me away?"

"Nope. Don't have a clue. Probably scaring you away is what's going on. From the things that happened, lights on, silhouettes in the windows, and slashed tires, I don't see someone means to harm you." He sipped his wine. "But I don't like the slashed tires business."

"Do you think Polly fell or was pushed off the widow's walk?"

"What, or who, put that bee in your bonnet? O'Reilly? Bunch of crap. Told him to let that idea go. No truth to it."

Joe was visibly agitated. Plowing his hand through his hair a giveaway. He was plowing vigorously. I could tell by watching and listening that he wasn't on the same wavelength as O'Reilly. Annie, the sleuth, took over. Maybe Joe was hiding something. I dropped the subject.

Our conversation kind of petered out and we finished our meal at the same time. Neither of us had room for dessert. Joe caught the waitress's eye and asked for the check. He pulled out his credit card, paid the bill then escorted me to my car. I thanked him for a pleasant evening, unlocked the door, and wriggled my tight-skirted body into the driver's seat.

Joe reached for my hand, took it in his, turned it over, and rubbed his index finger over the calluses on it. He let his index finger trace lazy circles in the sensitive hollow of my palm as he looked into my eyes.

Umm, Ummm, that palm petting of his sent electric zingers to places down south on my body that hadn't zinged for a long time. His sandalwood scent tickled my nose. I wondered if he smelled like that all over his bare skin. Yummy!

Joe smiled down at me and I was relieved that he wasn't a mind reader. My face felt hot. From past experiences I knew it would be ruby red. I couldn't meet Joe's eyes. He whispered, "See you later, Annie," then got in his car and drove away. After he was long gone, I was still sitting in my car in the parking lot. I shook my head but that didn't help clear the confusion I felt. I left Canton and drove to the apartment in Carterville on autopilot as I sorted through a muddle of what-ifs.

28

I SEARCHED FOR THAT DAMNED diary for over a week without success. After I ate lunch on Monday I lingered a short time at the kitchen table sipping the last of my coffee. I dreaded going back upstairs to work. I wasn't in a laboring frame of mind today. Mrs. B had left a few minutes earlier to make a trip into Canton for her weekly grocery shopping.

Taking a quick look around the kitchen I saw her purple bottomless-pit bag lying open on the counter. I ran over and pawed through it stirring up its contents as I searched for the diary. Yeah! It was there all right underneath what looked like every one of Mrs. B's earthly possessions. I grabbed the book and rushed to the table to read it. I thumbed the pages. The book fell open in the middle. I started reading.

12 August...1926

Today I went to an auction at the Snyder farm. I bid and won a delightful cherry wood spinning wheel and directed the moving man to place it in the third floor bedroom under the front window.

What a gloriously peaceful day today has been. Polly stays unusually quiet. It is always a blessing when she is obedient.

Carl remains at his family home in Sedalia, Missouri, for a long neglected visit. He is destined to return in November.

13 August…1926

Today has been another restful day. The workers came to do for us this morning. I wish I could have in house help but they upset Polly so when they are here. The house is being readied for Harry's visit in the morning. He comes to make plans with Polly about their wedding.

Not a bit too soon.

Polly's wedding dress hangs in the armoire. It has been fashioned from white satin and is of a simple design that can be let out if needed. She chose white lace for her train.

Polly looks like an angel in her finery.

14 August…1926

Today I murdered Harry.

My whole body went on alert. That was as much of the diary as I could read. I heard footsteps coming up the stairs to the back door. I knew it was Mrs. B. She was cussing in paragraphs. My heart thumped in my ears. I slammed the book shut, ran over and thrust it underneath the whole mess in Mrs. B's bottomless pit. I knew where it was now if I got another opportunity. I dashed back to the table, threw myself into a chair, and pretended to slurp coffee from my empty cup. Mrs. B yanked the back door open and rushed into the kitchen.

"Well Annie, what do you think about that?" she shouted.

"About what?" I shouted back, in a quick reaction to her forceful voice, then choked on the mouth full of spit my panic produced. *Yikes! Did she see me reading the diary?*

From the heat radiating off my face, I felt an enormous bright red sign across it flashing, "Guilty! Guilty! Guilty!"

"Didn't I tell you that I never leave any place without my bottomless pit? Well, I left it here with my car keys in it. I'm a real slow top today."

"Won't get very far without your keys will you?" I squeaked.

"What's wrong with you, Annie? You look like you've been sucking on a lemon or sat on a hot poker."

"This coffee warmed me up," I fibbed. Then worried if my tiny fib would need to adjust itself into a giant lie.

Mrs. B picked up her bag, slung it over one hefty shoulder. "Goodbye again," she said, and out the door she went.

Phew! That was a close one.

29

WHEN I LEFT THE APARTMENT at 6:50 that same evening to go over to the Carter house the sky was as black as ink. The wind howled in the tall oak trees and made clacking noises in their branches far above my head. I shivered and hugged myself as the cold ground crept up through the soles of my tennis shoes. The frigid wind wriggled its way up under my jacket. I was restless and uneasy.

I rushed through the back door of the Carter house, slammed it shut, and locked myself inside. I turned on the tap and drew a glass of water, drinking it in thirsty gulps. I took a Hershey bar out of my hidey-hole stash and peeled the brown paper off to get to the good stuff under the foil. I quit making paper noises and stood still. Did I hear footsteps overhead. Who, other than I, would be in the house this late at night, and why? I stood like a statue in one spot listening. When I didn't hear the noise again I decided it must have been the blustery wind that lay in wait to sneak in through the countless cracks in this old building. I hadn't been here in the house after dark before. I didn't like feeling as if I weren't alone.

When I'd made the decision to clean the chandelier at this late hour, my imagination must have shoved itself into high gear. I shook off all thoughts of boogey men lurking in the dark rooms waiting to pounce on me. Then I scolded myself for being frightened by an unidentified sound.

I decided to take a little extra time and clean the transom before I worked on the chandelier.

Moving the eight-foot wooden ladder away from the wall in the kitchen, I wrestled it out to and down the front hall. At the entry doors I stood it upright, released the safety latch, and popped it open as close as I could to the transom.

Years ago, mother invented a mixture she swore by for cleaning glass of any kind, especially cut glass. The concoction was a blend of ammonia cut with water with a few drops of laundry bluing added. That combination makes glass sparkle like nothing else will. I hooked the trigger handle of my squirt bottle of the mixture through one of the front loops of my jeans, and pushed a clean soft rag in my back pocket. Climbing the ladder I hummed my working song. I've never been able to whistle so often will hum the melody of "Whistle While you Work." It never sounds the same as when the dwarfs did it in *Snow White*. The words fooled around in my head.

After a squirt and a rub the stained glass transom colors sprang to life. The chandelier that hung from the center of the hall ceiling reflected the colors. The old-fashioned pastoral scene was eye-catching even on this dark night. I knew it would look spectacular on a clear day with the sun shining through it. The vibrant colors would bounce off the walls, ceiling, and floor. It was too cold to clean the outside tonight. Maybe I could get Willie to do it later.

Joe told me he intended to tear down the house and build tract homes to sell on the one city block where it now sat. I hated to see the window removed from its place where it undoubtedly gave years of pleasure to the Carter family. Some lucky person at the auction would bid right and haul it away to adorn a different home.

Tomorrow, I would look up its worth and add it to the hall inventory sheet.

I carried the ladder under the fixture in the parlor. With my active imagination I thought I could feel Polly's cobalt eyes watching me from her portrait. The hairs on the back of my neck stood on alert. I was definitely spooked tonight.

I'd been giving my flight-or-fight adrenaline rushes a serious work out lately.

The chandelier in here is an unusually large one. It held numerous make-believe candles with those small fancy bulbs that come to a point. Fashioned many years ago from brass and cut glass, it had held real candles before being converted to electricity. It tinkled pleasingly, like a wind chime, as I rubbed my damp cloth over the many dangling pieces of glass. I figured the chandelier to be worth about four thousand dollars. Some collector of the brilliant era would no doubt be thrilled to bid on it.

With the light switch toggled off at the wall and only the table lamps to see by, I worked from the outside to the inside of the piece. The years of grime clinging to the dangling prisms hadn't given the fixture its best look. It would soon be in mint condition. As my cleaning rag arrived at the center of the fixture I must have jostled one of the hanging pieces. A whole section of it fell onto the faded Oriental rug with a muffled tinkle.

I climbed down from the ladder, bent, and picked up what I thought was a part of the chandelier. As I gazed down at the sparkling piece nestled in the palm of my hand, I realized what it was. Polly's diamond necklace!

How in the hell did that get up there?

30

I RAN TO THE KITCHEN PHONE and punched in Joe's numbers. When he answered I shouted, "I found Polly's diamond necklace right here in the house."

He bellowed in my ear, "Hot damn, be right over," and slammed down the receiver.

I rushed to the large mirror hanging on the wall in that room, and positioned the diamonds around my neck, admiring how they looked on me. When I twisted my shoulders back and forth the stunning piece released a gazillion tiny lights. I felt like a queen or at the very least a princess. It hadn't been up there long enough to get dusty so it didn't need to be cleaned. I reluctantly took it off, held it over the pocket in my jeans and let it slither sensuously inside.

Joe arrived at the house in his best time ever, only fifteen minutes after I'd called. A grin spread across his lips and lit up his face as he came through the kitchen door. I pulled the necklace out of my pocket and wiggle-waggled it in front of his face.

Joe grabbed me around the waist, picked me up off the floor, and swung me in circles around and around. He was laughing like a child on his birthday morning.

He smelled like a brewery.

He let my feet touch the floor, steadied me. He took the necklace from my hand and slurred, "Iz a beautiful thing izn it, Annie? Whadaya think its worth?"

"I don't have a clue, Joe. I'm not an expert at appraising jewelry. You'll have to take it to someone who knows its value. I suggest getting three estimates, possibly even let Sotheby's in New York appraise it. Maybe, put it in one of their auctions. Take your time."

"I'll tell O'Reilly you found this. Jeez, thanks a million, Annie," Joe mumbled. He kissed my cheek, let the necklace slide into his jacket pocket and went out the back door on shambling feet.

I locked up and went back to the apartment feeling sad all of a sudden. To cheer myself up I called Venus and told her about finding the necklace. I asked if she wanted to come to Carterville and stay overnight.

Venus spit out such a loud "Yes," it crackled in my ear. "I've been bored out of my gourd lately."

We talked about trying the dance at the community center held here on Tuesday nights. I'd seen the woman I now thought of as Ron's grandmother entering the Community Center last week during the dance. If she was there I intended to corner her and pick her brains about Ron.

After the dance I planned on chatting up Venus about what's been happening here in Carterville. I needed her to help formulate a scheme for what I should do next. It always makes things clearer in my head when I use Venus as a sounding board. She has an analytical turn of mind and knows just how to organize my thoughts if they become muddled. She is also creative with zany ideas I would never think of in a million years.

Venus told me she couldn't wait to skip the light fantastic, whatever in the hell that meant. She volunteered to call Oscar to cover for her at the shop and would also ask him to cat-sit Sugar.

Ever the optimist, I found myself thinking about the possibility that my Mr. Right Guy could/would/might be at this dance. I'd been thinking, ever since my divorce, about not wanting to spend my senior years alone. I didn't want to turn into a Myrtle, the irritating woman who lives next door to me in Peoria. I think the reason she spends so much time spying on the neighbors is that she has no life of her own.

Since my divorce from an alcoholic and abusive husband last year I've been actively searching for my Mr. Right Guy. I've dated several Mr. Wrong Guys. There were tall men, small men, round men, lean men, handsome men, and not-so-handsome men. One of them, a blond Adonis, thought a sub-division was a math problem. Another guy, a redhead, thought espresso meant eight items or less. Then there was Jasper. Ah, Jasper! His prime entertainment was guzzling a six pack of beer while watching a bug-zapper do its work. After his beer cans were emptied he would walk his dog. They both watered the same tree.

When dating it seems as if I'd become a magnet for every boozer, loser, and user that graduated magnum cum laude from the College of Warp the Truth. I read a magazine article once titled "Do You Attract Weird Guys Like Flies?" Well yeah! That is what I do. Like I wear a T-shirt that reads "Use me-Abuse me-I like it." One section in that article gave hints about finding a compatible mate. I've used them all. None of their suggestions have been productive.

* * *

Venus arrived on Tuesday night, her Spanish heritage evident by the dress she wore. Venus looked gorgeous in a bright red, floor-length chiffon dress with layers of ruffles around the bottom. She had on a new pair of black dancing slippers instead of the high-top tennis shoes she usually paired with any ensemble. Her hair was pulled up on top of her head and she looked chic. When I asked about her new look, she told me that Nancy, the woman who manages the New to You clothing shop, told her that the dress was a 'happening fashion.'

I'd spent way too much time tonight getting ready for the dance. I wore one of my old favorites that was comfortable, black chiffon palazzo pants paired with an "I'm oh so feminine lacy white blouse." Of course, I wore the shoes that made me five foot five instead of five-two. I spiked my hair with spray so it stood straight up and pointy on top of my head, giving me another inch and a half in height. Stroking a favorite white flower perfume behind my ears, I clipped on rhinestone earrings.

I was dressed for man-hunting territory.

When Venus and I entered the double doors of the community center in Carterville, I scanned the room for a glimpse of the woman I assumed was Ron's grandmother. I didn't see her in the crowded room.

Venus and I paid the five-dollar fee for a night of dancing and had the back of our hand stamped with a CC by a little old lady with blue-white hair. She informed us that stamping was required in case we wanted to leave the dance then come back in again. She bent over and whispered in my ear, "a lot of hanky-panky goes on out there in those parked cars at break time."

A three-piece band was playing on a small raised dais to our left in the front corner of the room. Their instruments were trumpet, guitar and piano. The man with the trumpet stopped playing and began singing in a whiskey voice as Venus and I walked to the back of the room. The lights dimmed, the band played. The trumpet player sang one of my favorite songs, "Waltz Across Texas."

As the trumpet player sang those beautiful words the Fred Astaire and Ginger Rogers "Wannabees" swayed, swirled and dipped out on the dance floor. A large sphere suspended from the center of the ceiling rotated slowly. It sent myriad tiny sparkles swirling erratically over the dancers, the walls, and the gleaming wooden floor.

A tiny bar on the back wall the size of a minivan was doing a brisk business. A smorgasbord of men stood three deep competing noisily for the overwhelmed bartender's attention. Venus and I went to a table for twelve and sat in the last two empty folding chairs.

Hmmm, I'd already spotted three potential dance partners looking us over.

31

SWEATY PALM MET SWEATY PALM as a very tall man, six foot six if he was an inch, led me onto the floor for my first dance of the evening. He looked way down into my face and gave me a toothy smile. His soft gray eyes were gorgeous, and he had a beautiful tanned complexion, as if he spent a lot of time outdoors. He introduced himself as Tom. His hi-wader khaki pant-legs ended at the tops of his white work socks. His high gloss brown shoes seemed unfamiliar with his feet. He kept looking down at them every time he tripped. His black hair was in a traditional man's cut. It gleamed like patent leather. Tom and I struggled around the floor for what seemed like time without end. His lips moved to the count of a waltz tempo, one, two, three, one two, three.

Tom seemed like a very nice man but smelled week-old without a shower.

My next dance was with a man who turned out to be a really good dancer, easy to follow. Impeccably dressed, he wore a black suit, black dancing shoes and a spotless white shirt, with a red tie that had a small design in it.

When I was in his arms and close up I could see that the tie had, different colored matchbox cars embroidered on it. He looked pulled together except for the giant gold cuff links shaped like Lamborghini's.

He'd probably spent more mirror time tonight than I had.

He told me his name was Woody. I knew a man years ago that called his little man who lived behind his zipper that same name when it got excited. I worried about calling him Woody.

While we danced the perimeter of the floor I scanned the room looking for 'Ron's grandmother,' while listening to his conversation. It was all about him. He was a used car salesman from Canton. He'd dated more women than I could count on my cute little fingers and toes. He boldly swung me out then twirled me and looked me up and down.

As he whirled me back into his arms, he crushed me against his body and declared, "I'm ready for a new relationship."

Woody's silver and black wooly worm eyebrows shot up three inches on his forehead and disappeared into a serious comb over. He looked expectantly at me. Then his green eyes roamed my face, dropped lower, zeroed in, and did a stopover in my cleavage. I thought I'd have to run and get him a bib. When he peeled his eyes away from my boobs, he said, "I have a feeling this is your lucky day little lady."

Good God! The man was full of himself and full of something else too if he thought I'd be interested in his line of BS. The song we danced to finished.

He led me back to the table where Venus was sitting and announced in a loud voice, "If you come back next week, I'll ditch my date for you."

It looked like I could erase two more men from my list of a possible lifetime mate. *Yuck!*

"This is a good shindig," Venus said, as a gentleman bordering on Methuselah whisked her away to the dance floor. The expression on his face reminded me of a coyote at a rabbit convention.

I hadn't seen the woman I came here to talk to. I was tired but Venus was still going strong. She looked as happy as a fly in raison pie.

Would this night never end?

Finally! They played the song I'd been waiting to hear.

THE LAST DANCE
You can dance
Every dance with the guy who gives you the eye
Let him hold you tight

You can smile
Every smile for the man who held your hand
'neath the pale moonlight

But don't forget who's takin' you home
And in whose arms your gonna be
So darlin' save the last dance for me.

32

RIDING IN PINKY, VENUS'S CAR, after the dance, I asked her to be my sounding board while I designed a plan to get that elusive diary. Also, when I talked it out I might discover who was trying to frighten me away from the Carter house.

Venus, as my guest, was first in the shower, then I took my turn. Squeaky-clean, I pulled on a one-size-fits-all T-shirt. In the kitchen I poured us each a glass of homemade blackberry wine, compliments of Mr. B. I arranged the wine, a wedge of Asiago cheese and some saltines on a bent tray I'd unearthed from under the sink.

Okay, so what if I'm not Miss Suzy Homemaker of the month.

I sat in the old brown recliner in the bedroom while Venus got comfortable as my guest in the bed. Both pillows propping her up, a glass of wine poised in her hand, she wriggled underneath the covers. Venus said, "Ready, set, go," and pointed a finger at me.

That was all the encouragement I needed. I was primed with a load of questions nagging at me about the goings-on here in Carterville.

I jumped right in.

"I really feel that it's Mrs. B who's been trying to frighten me. She must have been the one who flattened the tires on my car too. But what would she have to gain by scaring me away? She's just Polly's caregiver. There's the puzzler. I can't see any rhyme nor reason for her to behave that way. Besides that, she denied all of it. I'm trying to understand why she'd behave in that manner. That's what I need to figure out."

I babbled on, but now that I'd started, I needed to get it all out. "I don't want to make enemies of the people here by asking questions. I need to take it slow, be on the lookout and focus on the people I've met here in Carterville."

Venus gave a mighty yawn and held out her glass for a refill.

I came back from the kitchen with her wine and resumed spilling my thoughts.

"I also question why she took that one diary in particular. Maybe I'll ask her to give it to me. After all, I am looking after Joe's interests—and his belongings.

"Venus, listen to my list of questions.

"Where did Mrs. B come from?

"How did it come about that she was hired to take care of Polly?

"Why did she stick it out for fifty years? My God! No one I've ever known has been on one job for that many years.

"Maybe she thought there would be something in the will for her.

"After that many years of service she probably expected a windfall."

I glanced at Venus. Her eyes were drooping.

"I need to think about that diamond necklace, too. Someone had to toss the thing up in that chandelier."

Venus said, "If I'd gotten my hands on it I sure wouldn't toss it up in a chandelier. I'd cash it in and fly off to the Riviera."

Still full of questions, I cried out, "Maybe it was Ron? It probably wasn't the grandmotherly woman I saw him with in Canton at that antique mall. I've never seen her over at the Carter house. Besides, she looks like a sweet old lady.

"At this point I'm starting to wonder about Joe, Venus. Though I don't know what he could possibly gain by scaring me away. After all he was the one who hired me in the first place."

"Sounds like you're narrowing the list of suspects, Annie. Any one else you think it might be?"

"Well, I did think about it being Mr. B at one time."

"I don't see that happening. He's dumber than a rock. Did I ever tell you he called me at the shop in Peoria the day after I was here last time? You know the day of Operation Diary."

"You're kidding."

"Mr. B wanted to take me to lunch. I told him no way, Jose. If that wife of yours caught us together she'd take a shovel to our heads then dig a hole big enough to bury both of us. That shut him up. He only made that one call."

"I suspect you're right about it not being him."

I started to tell Venus about reading the words in the diary where Sarah murdered Harry. I still thought I might have misread them. I'd tell her about it if—and when—I was able to read those actual words again.

"You know teamwork usually lightens a load, Annie. But let's talk some more in the morning. I'm sleepy."

"Well, okay, but I've been wondering . . ." I realized Venus was snoring softly.

I went to the living room, flattened my body out on the lumpy couch but its lumps didn't fit mine. Dropping my head on the spare skimpy, stinky pillow, I pulled the blankets up to my chin.

The questions continued to circle in my head. Now I needed answers.

33

VENUS AWOKE AT FIVE O'CLOCK. She planned on eating at a restaurant halfway between here and home. Her visit had been a nice break in my routine.

* * *

Mrs. B's menus never vary from week to week. I knew that today, being Wednesday, lunch would be a fried Spam sandwich and a cup of canned soup. I'm a sucker for Spam. Interrupting my work earlier than usual, I went down to the kitchen for lunch and caught Mrs. B red-handed. She was sitting at the table with her back to me reading the diary I'd been searching for.

She must have heard me as I came into the room. "I'll have your lunch ready in a jiffy, Annie."

I walked over and sat down in my usual place at the head of the table. When I looked up again the book was nowhere in sight. She must have hidden it somewhere in this room. She didn't have enough time to stash it anywhere else. I'd seen it in her hands. She didn't leave the kitchen. Next thing I knew, I didn't see it in her hands.

Her huge bottomless pit was on the table next to me where I sat. She didn't put it in there or I would have seen that.

After lunch Mrs. B left for the day. I searched for the journal. Where in the hell could she have stashed it? There were so many places she could have hidden it. I began poking into nooks, crannies, alcoves, and corners. I rummaged through the dish cupboards. I looked in the freezer and refrigerator, inside cereal boxes, behind canned goods in the pantry, the broom closet, inside the mop bucket, picked through the mess under the sink, then gave up for the day. I'd wasted two valuable hours searching for that damned diary.

I wouldn't be content unless I explored the contents of that particular book but would have to quit looking for it now. Persevere I would, later. Pouring water in the pot I started two cups of coffee brewing to take with me upstairs then decided to fix a piece of cinnamon toast to nibble on.

Going to the counter by the stove where the breadbox sits, I reached inside and took out the half a loaf of white bread, removed a slice, and popped it down into the toaster. When I started to deposit the loaf of bread back in the box I saw, resting on the bottom, Sarah's elusive diary. I grabbed it, clutching it to my chest as if it might grow wings and fly away. I ran up the servant stairs to the attic and shoved the diary down inside of the box of dollies, all the way to the bottom. I wasn't taking any chances that Mrs. B would come back into the kitchen as before. I intended to return here tonight after I finished working for the day. I was going to read the damned thing with no more interruptions.

The grandfather clock in the hall was ticking close to three, the hour Ron was scheduled to burn trash. I wanted to be gone from the kitchen when he got here so I wouldn't have to interact with him.

I hurried from the attic down the servants' stairs and poured coffee into the thermos, spread butter on the hard piece of toast, and sprinkled cinnamon and sugar on it. Then I took both energy fuels, and a cup upstairs to the second floor where I relaxed in Polly's wing chair by the cold fireplace.

The room smelled musty so I went to the window and opened it wide to blow out the stale odors.

Thoroughly enjoying my impromptu picnic, I considered the pros and cons of coming back over here tonight to read in the attic. The pros won. I felt as if the information in that one diary might answer my questions. Those words of Sarah's had haunted me ever since I'd read them. "Today I murdered Harry." I couldn't quite make myself believe that was what I'd read.

When I heard Ron drive up to the house I went to the open window and looked out as he stepped under the roof of the back porch. He disappeared from sight. Without delay he came back into view again carrying a pile of trash, which he stacked in the empty wheelbarrow used for transporting things back and forth. Ron pushed the load out to the burn area. He hadn't had enough time to pilfer anything from inside the house. Flicking his Zippo he lit the rubbish. The smoke caught on the wind, and billowed in through the open window where I stood.

I eased the window shut but must have made enough noise that Ron heard me. He looked up at the window, staring right where I showcased myself. If I read the look on his face accurately, he didn't like me any better than I liked him. He jerked up a rake, stirred the smoldering embers then dumped a bucket of water over them. He jumped in his truck, glared up at me, and spit small rocks and dirt as he zoomed down the drive. Good riddance!

All the time I'd spent looking for that diary could have been put to better use working upstairs. I'd finished inventorying in the attic and the downstairs rooms. I had maybe another hour of work up here on the second floor. Tomorrow I could begin on the third floor servant rooms. They were in an unholy mess.

Tonight I promised myself I'd go to the attic and read that diary.

34

BY SEVEN OCLOCK THAT EVENING, I'd finished my shower and dinner. Snatching up the heavy-duty flashlight from the kitchen counter, I left the apartment and locked the door. Halfway down the stairs, I turned around, went back up, checked the door again to be doubly sure it was locked. Satisfied, I proceeded in the direction of the Carter house.

The black night was daunting and real spoooooky, so I flicked the button on my flashlight. *Ah*! With that wide bright beam of light I immediately felt less defenseless.

I shook myself and said out loud, "Grow up Annie." The words didn't help but the sound of my own voice was somehow comforting. The entire world seemed to be holding its collective breath...waiting...waiting... waiting...for an unknown something to happen.

It was so quiet that the crunching of my feet on the gravel pathway echoed, making me think someone or something was dogging my tracks. I twirled around rapidly and raked the beam of light back and forth like a lighthouse beacon. I saw nothing unusual. Nothing behind me that appeared out of place. But if someone, or something, was stalking me, the flashlight was lighting up their prey! I switched the light off and laid tennis shoe rubber toward the back door.

When I reached the door, the momentum of my sprint hurled me against the door. I twisted the knob while launching my body against it, expecting it to open. *Crap!* It was locked! Pain attacked my shoulder. I needed to unlock the damned door, not flatten it. I was glad no one was around to question my lack of common sense.

Juggling the flashlight I fished the house key out of my jacket pocket, inserted it in the keyhole, twisted it and heard a click. When I walked into the kitchen it was cozy and warm, a safe place at last. Phew! That trip over here drained a lot of the starch out of my backbone.

In the middle of the lit kitchen I caught a glimpse of something, out the corner of my eye. A face in the window over the sink stared at me from outdoors. I squealed, leaped in the air, primed to run away. Then I realized my own face reflecting from the window glass had just scared the hell out of me.

TV shows make detective work look easy. I was finding out it's not so simple in real life, especially if you're afraid of your own reflection.

Whimp...Whimp...Whimp...protested my gray matter when I thought about the known comforts at the apartment, compared to unknown terrors in this house after dark. The word defined how I felt. Terrified.

Nothing feels quite so lonely and intimidating as a silent house when you are alone. All things seem simpler—and safer—when another person stands beside you.

I grabbed a candle and some matches out of the junk drawer in the kitchen and a saucepan from the lower cupboard. As I cautiously began the climb up the servant staircase, every protesting moan my footfalls created on the wooden treads sounded like a shout announcing my presence.

Nothing ventured! Nothing gained! I surged forward and upward, boldly lighting my way with the flashlight. When I arrived at the attic I made my way to the dolly's box and reached way down inside. My fingers found the worn edges of the diary. I pulled it up from the bottom of the box. Easing myself to the floor, I leaned against the furnace's chimney to capture some of its warmth.

I lit the candle and tipped it slightly so melted wax dripped into the saucepan, then I anchored the candle in the melted wax until it hardened enough to stay secure upright. Placing the pan on the bottom of an upside down box I clicked off the flashlight.

The drafts sneaking in through the cracks in the attic flirted with the sheets that I'd draped over the windows when I finished cataloging this area. The currents of air teasing the candle flame produced tall and short, fat and skinny, ghostly shapes. The eerie figures rose and fell in a slow-moving undulating dance over the bare rafters to create a cluster of otherworldly special effects.

I gulped noisily and refused to look at the phantasms again.

In my hands Sarah's elusive diary fell open at the same page I'd last read as though it knew exactly where I wanted to look. I began skimming the words.

Oh, my God! *I had* seen those damning words. There had been a murder in this house.

35

14 August...1926
   Today I murdered Harry.

My thoughts reeled as images coursed through my mind. I took a deep breath and continued reading.

15 August ...1926
   As I think on what yesterday wrought it seems a dream unfolding. What I did plays over and over in my mind. I can see we three seated in the parlor by the fireplace. We talk about Polly's condition. Harry smiles cruelly as he breaks Polly's heart with the words, "I will not marry you. I will not be burdened with a mad woman the rest of my life." I tremble with the rage I feel at this man. With the strength of ten I grab the fireplace poker, swing it, and strike Harry on the back of his head. The sound that makes is one I

will never forget, like that of a pumpkin exploding. Blood splatters over the front of the mantelpiece. Harry falls to the rug. His eyes stare vacantly. He no longer breathes.

Polly screams. I slap her face repeatedly until she is quiet. I have never before struck Polly. She does not say a word. I tell her, "You must help me, the police will come and take me away from you. I will be hanged. You will never see me again."

Polly and I roll Harry's body up in the middle of the rug he fell on. Together we tug and pull the rug with Harry's body inside. Polly and I drag it from the parlor, through the kitchen, down the porch steps. Once outside we pull our burden down the path to the cooling house. We frantically dig a hole in the dirt floor, roll Harry into it, and cover him over with the dirt. I pull Polly to her room where I lock her inside. Then I drive Harry's truck to the back of our fence line to hide it from prying eyes.

He was leaving town and would not wed Polly.

August 20...1926

Five days have passed since confiding in you, diary. Polly has become nearly unmanageable. I have had to sedate her with opiates. She screams and pulls large patches of hair out from her head.

I tell family and friends that Harry has been called away on business and he and Polly have had to postpone their wedding day.

I keep Polly locked in her room.

August 21...1926

I cannot keep sedating Polly. I am thinking that it may harm the baby that grows inside her. I must keep her hidden until she delivers, then place the child in an orphanage.

What will I tell Carl when he returns in November?

I gently closed the book on Sarah's words. I couldn't read any more tonight. The words blurred one into another. I brushed away tears running freely down my cheeks. My heart ached for Sarah and Polly's anguish, even after so many years had passsed.

It would do me no good to sit here in the cold attic, pondering the many questions of this puzzle when I could go back to the apartment and think in warm comfort. As I stood up I thought I heard the sound of someone entering the house through the front door? Who would be downstairs at this hour?

I heard shuffle, clump, shuffle, clump, as though someone took a step then yanked a heavy object. Visions of Sarah and Polly dragging Harry's body filled my mind.

After I blew out the candle, I shivered from the cold, the dark, and my fear.

I hadn't thought to tell anyone I was coming here tonight and had left my cell phone in the apartment. If a person here in the house was bent on doing me harm, I prayed they wouldn't think to look up here. Why hadn't I thought about the possibility that the light from the candle might be noticeable from the attic windows, though I had covered them with old sheets. I eased myself to the floor and sat motionless for what seemed hours but probably was no more than fifteen minutes. I concentrated on breathing slow, and shallow. I intended to wait until the intruder left.

Finally I heard the squealing sound again as the front door opened, then closed. Whoever had been down there must have left. I did a butt walk as quietly as I could to the top of the stairs, and hid the book back in the box of dollies.

Able to see by the moonlight through the windows on each of the landings I eased myself down the steps by sitting on one then lowering myself to the next one.

Determined not to turn on my flashlight, though I needed its light, I made it to the kitchen in that manner. I stood up and pussyfooted across the floor, eased out the back door and quietly locked it. Then I ran to the carriage house as if the hounds of hell were chasing me.

When I reached the apartment I unlocked it, rushed in and took my first deep gulp of air for the night.

36

UNABLE TO SLEEP after I went to bed, I flipped and flopped well into the early hours of morning. The last time I checked Big Ben his hands pointed to three-twenty. I felt as if I'd taken a seat on top of several sticks of dynamite, and someone was about to strike a match.

I couldn't shut off my brain. It was processing one question in particular that was sickening, but one I needed to think about. The possibility that Sparky had been bringing bits and pieces of Harry's burial site to Joe and me. Was he fetching us scraps of material from Harry's clothing or could it be little pieces of the rug he'd been wrapped in? I didn't know how fast rugs deteriorated in that length of time, or clothing. The scraps Sparky had been bringing us looked more like fabric instead of a rug.

Was that vintage truck in the garage the very same one that Harry used in his bootlegging business? How was that possible after so many years? Was that the same truck Sarah drove to the fence line after she murdered Harry? Then all those other unanswered questions…

Who was it trying to frighten me away when I first came to Carterville?

Why had someone gone to such lengths to chase me off?

Why didn't Mrs. B want me to read that particular diary?

Why did she choose to hide this one from prying eyes and none of the others?

She hadn't murdered Harry and was only a caregiver, wasn't she?

Should I call Joe tonight and let him know about the murder?

Did I trust Joe? Was he the one frightening me, for some implausible reason that I couldn't imagine.

Was it Ron? I hadn't ruled him out.

Was it some person I hadn't met or thought of yet?

Should I tell Chief O'Reilly?

My brain felt like mush with so many unanswered questions whirling around. Since it was so late and I couldn't do anything till morning anyway, I decided to try to sleep on it.

At seven o'clock Thursday morning, I stumbled groggily to the phone and caught sight of myself in the mirror. Yikes! I seriously needed a trim. My hair came to a point on top of my head again, my benchmark for a haircut. It's not a pretty sight when my unruly hair turns me into a cone-head.

I dialed Joe's number. A woman answered. I thought the voice sounded like Monica's, the waitress from the Donut Hole. Scratch another potential man from my list as a senior citizen companion. He drank too much to suit me anyway.

The woman yelled, "Joe, it's that woman."

When he came on the line I told him, "I need to talk with you, Joe."

"Can it wait till tomorrow evening, Annie? Got a bunch of crap happening here I need to deal with."

I thought about Harry's family. They'd probably speculated for years about what had become of him. In spite of everything, he was somebody's son or brother. The exposure of Harry's murder had been put on hold for so many years, however, that I couldn't see what harm could result from waiting one more day.

"I suppose it can wait till tomorrow but no longer."

"I'll come by Friday evening at six."

"Bring Sparky!" I shouted before he could hang up.

My plan was to turn the dog loose on the grounds so he would run and do his favorite thing here, dig. That would lead us to the place where he'd found those bits of cloth. I shuddered when I thought about what we might find. Everything to do with unearthing Harry's remains would be put on hold until Joe and Sparky came by tomorrow evening.

I had only one more night to lie awake and fret.

The next morning I went to the third floor of Carter house and began inventorying the mess waiting for me there. I started my workday in that small front bedroom to see if it would still, by some miracle, have that cherry wood spinning wheel I'd read about in Sarah's diary.

The clutter along the walls reached to the lowered ceilings in the corners of the room. The ceilings of Victorian houses were built lower in servants' quarters to save on material costs. Also to remind the servants that they were a lower class of people. I created a circle of open space in the center of the floor by moving several boxes of miscellaneous memorabilia that had been accumulating in this room for years.

After pushing and pulling several heavy boxes of glassware to the cleared spot, I could see that they effectively had screened off the spinning wheel, which still sat under the window. It was a beautiful piece and I would have to look up the particulars later. I'd never had a spinning wheel to sell in the shop nor had I ever seen one. No information sprouted in my head to harvest. I polished the cherry wood with a special restorative paste wax that antique dealers use. The wheel didn't seem to have any dryness. The lovely old piece gleamed like new wood when I finished.

After that chore, I went to the cleared space and unfastened the dusty flaps on several heavy boxes of glassware. I ooohhed and ahhhhed as I took out each piece of cut glass and held it up to sparkle in the sunshine, then gently placed it on the floor. There were fancy pieces here that I'd never seen before, some bowls, pitchers, and numerous small items of cut glass from the brilliant era. They'd all been carefully wrapped in old newspapers that I removed and tossed out in the hall. I thought I'd probably display these glass pieces at the auction in the parlor on a long table covered with blue cloth. I intended to position them underneath the chandelier for the magnificent sparkle effect it would create.

Cut glass is exactly what the name implies. The more angles scored into a piece, the more it will glitter. It's also heavy, with thirty to fifty percent lead in each piece. When held in the palm of a hand, cut glass will ring with a bell-like tone when flicked with a finger. If it doesn't ring, it probably will have a crack along a major cut or it could possibly be only pressed glass.

I let my fingers do the authenticity telling. I picked up a large bowl in the palm of my left hand, closed my eyes, and flicked it with a finger. It produced a bell-like resonance. Then I felt around the outside of the piece with my fingers for sharpness of the cuts. Once you feel an imitation versus the real thing it's easy to differentiate between the real and the imitation. This bowl was dazzling in its brilliance and beautiful bell tone, and the cut edges were very, very sharp.

Hundreds of companies produced thousands of patterns over the past years and it takes an expert in that field to authenticate them. These were the real deal. All of the pieces I unwrapped this morning looked to be in mint condition, meaning they were never used. Several were signed "Libbey" and one had a "Hawkes' logo, both companies in the glass business. Those signatures are all acid-stamped. The ones I found were located on the bottom inside centers of the bowls. When authenticating, one must get to the proper lighting and turn the piece at many different angles to locate other places where a stamped mark might be. The logos are extremely hard to find. There had never been a designated place back then for signatures, so an old piece might be marked anywhere, at the marker's discretion.

It was a half-hour until lunchtime. I was hungry and needed coffee so decided to go down to the kitchen a little early. I went out into the hall and started to gather the newspapers that the cut glass pieces had been wrapped in. I planned on taking them down with me to put in the burn pile.

A picture and a headline caught my eye. The heading in the Fulton County newspaper was big, bold, and black:

CODY BROTHERS GANG SEIZED IN BEARDSTOWN

I recalled the fascinating stories that Muley, my father, told me years ago about the Cody brothers' reign of terror in Peoria during bootlegging days.

Under the header was a full body picture of the three brothers. Big John stood on the left, Harry in the middle, with Little Earl on his right. They were all sort of leaning towards each other and Harry had his arm around Little Earl's shoulder. The clothes they wore were typical of what my father said the well-dressed gangster had worn in those days. In the picture the Cody brothers had on fancy business suits, fedoras on their heads cocked at a two-eleven angle, and pulled low over their eyes.

This, then, was what Polly's fiancé had looked like. As I studied the picture of Harry Cody standing between his two brothers I could have sworn I knew him or had seen him somewhere. But that was impossible. The paper was dated August 20, 1926. In the picture Harry looked like he was well over six-foot tall, and stocky with broad shoulders. He and his brothers all stood with their feet turned outward giving them an awkward, graceless look. The article read:

In 1919, the 18th Amendment ratified prohibition of the manufacture and sale of alcohol. That amendment opened an era of large-scale organized crime in Illinois to supply bootleg alcohol and bathtub gin. The bootleggers look on the amendment as if it were a street paved of gold. To this day the sale of bootleg alcohol is rampant.

Approximately half of the fifty members of the Cody brother's gang have been arrested and jailed, with the exception of Harry Cody, who was last seen in Beardstown in August of this year. He is six-foot-six inches, long limbed, with dark hair and is known to be dangerous. If you see him contact the Peoria Police Department.

Twenty-one gang members were seized in a raid yesterday in the small town of Beardstown, Illinois. It is a well-known fact that the gangsters will often hide in houseboats on the Illinois River.

Some gang members bragged about law enforcement trying unsuccessfully again and again to capture them. The gangsters joked too often, too loud, and to the wrong people about a built-in indicator they had for announcing trouble when they were in that small town. It seems that when someone approaches their houseboat, the enormous quantity of frogs on the Illinois River banks cease their monotonous croaking. The sudden quiet alerts the gangsters that someone is in the vicinity and gives them ample time to escape further down into Little Egypt, a well-known moniker for the southern third of Illinois.

I was keyed up about finding the picture of Harry and his brothers. The article was longer and I wanted to read the rest of the story, but put it on hold for now. After hand ironing the newspapers that had been scattered over the floor, I piled them in a stack to take with me to the apartment to show to Joe tonight.

37

WHEN I FINISHED WORKING for the day at Carter house it was five o'clock on Friday so I rushed to the apartment. Joe was going to arrive at six. I put a pot of coffee on and made a sandwich out of potato salad on rye bread. Years ago I discovered that a ham slice, piled on with potato salad between two slices of bread—bingo! An easy stand-up dinner. I was out of ham but the potato salad sandwich was pretty damned tasty without it.

I crammed the last bite in my mouth when I heard Joe and Sparky outside on the landing. Joe tapped on the door. Sparky barked. I let them both in.

The dog made a beeline to the kitchenette and lapped up water from the pan I keep filled for him there. When he finished he jumped up on the couch and settled himself. Joe and I stood by the door like two dolts and watched Sparky make himself at home. When you have an animal you love they soon become almost like a child to you. Joe and I laughed as we looked at each other.

"Well, the three-legged kid has settled in now. Let's talk. What do you need to ask me? What's up, Annie?"

I asked him to sit at the table and poured each of us a cup of coffee. Taking a deep breath, I began. "This will take a while so please be patient. I have questions that need answers. And some information for you I've discovered about your Aunt Polly.

"Yep?"

"Was Sarah Carter Polly's mother?"

"How do you know Sarah's name?"

"I'll tell you that later. The first thing I need to know is, how did that old truck down in the garage under the apartment get there?"

"Found that truck years ago. Way out back along the fence line by the next street. Covered over with vines. Called my buddies. We hacked the vines away then pushed the truck into the garage. Didn't know what to do with it then—or now. Haven't taken the time to mess with it. It's been sitting there probably twenty years. Why do you need to know about that, Annie?"

"Wait just a bit more and you'll see."

I got up and went to the bedroom, brought out the recently missing diary, and laid it on the table. Pointing to it, I said, "I found a large number of these journals that Sarah, Polly's mother, wrote years ago. They were hidden in a secret compartment in one of the armoires in Polly's room. I brought all of them over here to the apartment and began reading, then one was missing." I pointed again to the diary. "This one was missing."

"But how…? Where was it?"

"How I tracked it down is a long story. I won't bore you right now with the details of my search. I'll fill you in later."

"Is there something written in the diary you think I should know? Spit it out, Annie."

"Right!" I told him about Sarah murdering Harry Cody, that she and Polly buried him in a place called the cooling house here on the property.

When I finished, Joe sat speechless, not moving a muscle and with his lips parted, looking as if he were trying to swallow but couldn't. Totally spaced out. I clapped my hands to make a loud noise as I tried to get a reaction. Sparky jumped down from the couch and laid his head on Joe's knee. Joe automatically reached down to stroke him, then he shook his head as he seemed to recover.

The enormity of what I'd just told him must have sunk in. He jumped up out of his chair so fast he knocked it over. His face turned the color of beet juice. God, I hoped he wasn't having a stroke.

He asked in a slow, low growling voice, "Sarah murdered Harry and she and Polly buried him out in back here? Is that what you're telling me?"

'That's right, Joe. That's what I said." I flipped open the book and pointed to the words I thought he needed to see to understand the truth of what I'd said.

Joe just stared at me, then sat back down. I watched as he read.

After he finished reading about the murder, he slammed the diary shut and threw it across the table.

"The reason I wanted you to bring the dog tonight, Joe, is that I've been thinking that maybe those pieces of cloth Sparky keeps fetching to us may be from the burial site. Maybe parts of the rug, but I suspect those pieces are more likely material from Harry's clothing. I was hoping that if we let Sparky off his leash he would lead us to the place where he's been digging."

"This is something I don't need right now, but... come on, we'll do it. My life is so screwed up, what's another nasty-assed thing added to my list? Monica says she's pregnant. Wants to keep the baby. Wants to get married."

That was a whole lot more information than I wanted to hear.

We put on our coats and Joe carried Sparky. I grabbed my flashlight, and down the stairs we three went. At the bottom step Joe bent and put the dog on the ground. Sparky took off with his odd looking run in the direction he usually headed. Joe and I followed. Sparky ran to a location where there had once been a building but now only the concrete outline of its foundation was revealed.

Sparky was doing a balancing act with his one good back leg. He was frantically digging in the dirt where the outbuilding had once been. Joe and I hurried to watch Sparky. I shined the flashlight on his chosen spot. A bone protruded from the ground. I jumped back with a shriek, bumped into Joe, and ran ten feet away from what I'd seen, my body trembling.

Joe came over to me and took the vibrating flashlight from my hand. He patted me on the back, saying, "Breathe, Annie, breathe deep."

That helped! I sucked in some badly needed air. Joe went to where Sparky now sat watching us with his head cocked to one side. Joe shined the light in the hole. I heard his sharp intake of breath and "God damn it!"

Joe hooked Sparky on his leash and pulled him away from the mound of dirt that he'd dug up. "Saw what looked like the same cloth Sparky's been bringing us. Did you see it, Annie?"

"Yes. Did you see the bone?"

"Yeah! Let's go to the apartment. Gotta call Chief O'Reilly."

* * *

O'Reilly arrived without lights or siren, at Joe's request. The two headed straight off to Sparky's digging place. The dog and I watched from the window of the apartment. The men stayed out there for a good twenty minutes. I could see the light bobbing around but had no wish to join them.

When they returned, O'Reilly screwed up his hornet chewing face and said, "I need to see that diary Joe tells me has information about a murder written in it, and the location of the body. By the looks of things out there in the woods I'd have to say that's not a recent burial. Looks like a real old skeleton."

"The diary is on the table," I told him.

"I'll need to take it with me tonight, Annie," O'Reilly said. "I have to call the medical examiner in Canton to come and have a look. I'll try to meet him early in the morning. The ME may have to call in a forensic anthropologist to verify the age and identity. But with written confirmation of a murder that took place years ago, the ME should be enough."

38

A BEEHIVE OF ACTIVITY took place in the woods out back at Carter house over the weekend, and again on Monday. I wasn't advancing very speedily in my role of amateur sleuth. I pretty much stayed away from the spot where the police were digging up Harry's body. Not that I wanted to, but because I'd been told by Chief O'Reilly, not so politely either, to butt out and then again by Officer Kidd, the baby-faced little twerp. I really wanted to look around inside that mobile crime scene unit. I was damned pissed off but had to satisfy myself with the news I caught on TV— and second hand information Joe doled out to me.

On Tuesday morning, the activity under the oaks had settled down. The mobile unit housing the equipment used in the investigation was the first to leave. No more to-ing and fro-ing from the four vans of people and all of the tools it takes to unearth bones. The police finally removed the yellow tape from the site where Harry's body had been unearthed.

Much later Joe told me that the medical examiner had found buttons and coins from the era when Harry Cody would have been alive. They also found a gold ring Joe said had "a diamond in it the size of Rhode Island." Must have been a real biggie. I would've given my eyeteeth to get a look at it.

Joe told me the ME said the bones were undoubtedly Harry Cody's. The autopsy revealed his death was the result of a skull fracture and had been caused by a blunt instrument consistent with a fireplace poker, just like the diary said. The police located several members of Harry's family and took DNA samples from them to confirm their findings. After the ME releases the remains they'll send the bones to the next of kin for proper burial.

After the police and reporters left Tuesday afternoon, curiosity led me over to the site.

All I could see was a large gaping hole in the ground. It smelled and looked like plain old black dirt. *Big damned deal!*

* * *

At least I'd accomplished a lot of work on the third floor of the Carter house over these past days. I looked forward to Thanksgiving dinner at Mrs. B's with Joe in two days' time, not for the food, but for the company. I wondered if his new dilemma with Monica might change things. Joe told me he'd escaped the wedding noose for sixty years and was old enough to be Monica's grandfather. Nevertheless, I thought he seemed excited about the prospect of being a father for the first time. They planned on a wedding soon, to beat the stork.

I'd been itching to read more in that diary after the police released it to Joe.

When I asked him about it he handed it to me. "Here, knock yourself out." He'd been surly with me, as if he blamed me because his aunt murdered Harry. I was only the bearer of bad news. I felt like telling him, "Don't kill the messenger."

That Tuesday night I curled up on the couch in the apartment and read more from the diary that he'd returned to me. There wasn't much else in it of interest. I found only mundane facts about life in 1927. And that Carl Carter, Polly's father and Sarah's husband had been killed in a farming accident when he'd visited his family in Sedalia. He never even knew about Polly's baby or Harry's murder.

There wasn't anything else of value written in that diary so I put it away and took the 1928 journal from the closet. I hit the information jackpot in a later section.

1 September 1928

After many trips these past five weeks to visit the orphanage in East Peoria I have decided to take Bernice there. I will leave for adoption the only grandchild that I am ever likely to have . I cannot control Polly's fits of wild behavior any longer. The physical acts of cruelty she accomplishes when I'm not in the room with her and the child I can no longer ignore. God alone knows what mental harm has been done to Bernice. I struggle daily to keep the child safe from her own mother. Bernice trembles and weeps if Polly comes near her.

2 September 1928

Today I took a snapshot of Bernice sitting in her little oak rocking chair before I taking her to the orphanage. I pledge that every time I look at that empty chair I will say a prayer for her safety and happiness.

Little Bernice clung to me when I passed her to Mother Superior at the orphanage. I peeled her little hands away from my skirt and ran out the door as I listened to that baby screaming for me, Gamma, Gamma. My heart is filled with sadness and I feel as if it has been emptied of any joy I've ever known. Sorrowful is the battle I engage in with myself. I want to return to that place and bring Bernice home but know I cannot.

3 September 1928

Today I have been reliving Bernice's birth on July 15 of last year with only me to attend Polly. I sent for Dr. Miller, our family physician since Carl and I wed. He hurried to the house but the baby arrived before him. The birthing was over. He filled in the certificate. I named the child Bernice after my mother.

Through all of the birth process Polly only whimpered with the pain that I'm sure she felt. She refused to speak a word. Her labor lasted for three hours only. A short time, I think. Polly seemed bewildered at what was happening to her body. When the baby arrived I placed it in her arms with the hope that she would welcome the tiny red wrinkled body. She screamed and threw the baby on the floor like she did with her dollies when she grew tired of them. Dr. Miller examined the child and told me that a baby is very flexible and he saw no damage by Polly's actions.

I have but the one picture of little Bernice to treasure for the rest of my life.

There'd been no other entry in the diary pertaining to the baby, but I now had a starting point to work from. I knew for a fact that a home for unwed mothers still exists in East Peoria. I went into the bedroom and took from the top of the dresser the picture that had fallen from the pages of one diary when I first started reading. I now felt sure this was the picture of baby Bernice that Sarah snapped on that long-ago day when she took her to the orphanage. I'd found pleasure in looking at that sweet-faced baby many times. I wondered what had become of baby Bernice.

It hadn't escaped me that the name Bernice looked a lot like the Berni, minus the ce, that Polly scratched in the dirt as she lay dying.

I left a message on Joe's answering machine telling him that I'd be going to Peoria, but intended to be back on Wednesday around noon. I also told him I worked extra time this past weekend while the police were out in back digging up bones.

I had some free time coming so thought I'd play detective again.

39

I DROVE TO PEORIA and slept in my own bed that night. It felt heavenly.

Wednesday at six I was up, dressed and on my way to McDonald's on Western Avenue for a sausage biscuit and a cup of coffee. I sat in a booth and ate hurriedly. Taking a second coffee with me, I drove over the bridge into East Peoria. When I arrived at St. Mary's home for unwed mothers and attached orphanage, it was still only seven forty-five. The information I'd found in the phone book last night said they opened at eight.

When I parked in front of the home, I scrunched down behind the steering wheel, holding the coffee cup in my hands as I tried to draw warmth through the Styrofoam container.

Looking over the place from my car, I saw the grounds were well tended with a variety of super tall trees around the buildings. A testament to the many years the facility had been here. Branches held a few tenacious leaves but were almost naked at this time of the year. Religious statues of saints I couldn't name dominated the scene.

With so many statues placed what seemed willy-nilly, I wondered if they were cheaper when bought by the dozen.

The building that housed unwed mothers and orphans had been constructed from red bricks that faded over the years to an attractive soft yellowish pink. St. Mary's main building was a two-story rambling affair that looked like it had been added onto over the years. Probably as their housing needs grew so did the building. I could hear, then see, an explosion of fifty or more bundled-up children of every size, shape, and race, erupting from a side door. The children sprinted to a play area on the east portion of the grounds. There were slides, swings, monkey bars, and what had once been my favorite as a child, a contraption I'd called a Go-A-Round.

Several children ran to the ride and set it in motion. They spaced themselves evenly around a wooden platform, running as they pushed it. When it got up to a speed where their short legs couldn't move any faster, all of the children jumped aboard and rode till it slowed to a stop. I remembered playing on the Go-A-Round until I got dizzy, tired, or it ceased to be fun. From the screaming and laughter coming from the playground I could tell the children were having a blast.

Jarringly, the scene on the opposite side of the street was ghetto-like. A run-down section of town had invaded East Peoria's inner city years ago. Long rows of two-story concrete block structures housed the poor. The place looked as if the inhabitants living there were long past caring about where or what they lived in. Faded curtains flipped and flapped from broken windows, taking on a life of their own as they seemed to wave at rubbish-strewn yards. Papers, garbage and dirt blew in eddies, stirred up by little gusts of wind.

Randomly placed sofas and chairs, once someone's living room furniture, had accumulated in the unkempt yards, their innards erupting from seams. One of the dirt-colored couches sitting along the curb opposite the orphanage held several pre-school children huddled together, sharing their warmth. Hungry eyes gazed longingly across the street at the orphan children laughing and playing.

We natives of Illinois can smell a snowstorm approaching. One was definitely on its way. I wanted to be back in Carterville before the roads turned treacherous. The blustery winds had become more forceful these past fifteen minutes as I sat in the car waiting for the orphanage to open. It wouldn't be long now before large wet flakes of snow would fall from the pewter-colored skies to hide everything under a blanket of the pristine white stuff.

I hurried up the sidewalk to the main entrance of St. Mary's outsized, carved, double wooden doors. They opened on silent hinges as I pushed to enter a cavernous hallway. My echoing footsteps were the only sounds I could hear, except for the peck-peck of a typewriter.

Directly opposite the entry was a long granite counter with a smallish woman sitting in front of a dilapidated typewriter. She had a pinched face and snow-white hair done up in a bun. On the lapel of her jacket were two identification pins. One read "Dorothy," the other "Information." That's what I was here after. I stepped up to the counter in front of her. We made eye contact, and her smile relaxed the brackets framing her mouth.

She asked in a soft voice, "May I help you?"

I smiled in return. "My name is Annie McMuffit. All I want is some information about a little girl adopted from here, probably in 1928 or possibly '29."

"You'll need to see Sister about that." She pointed to a long wooden bench sitting along the wall. "Please be seated over there. I'll call Sister Bridgett to come and talk to you." She picked up her phone.

I was too far away to hear what she said. I assumed she was notifying someone at the other end of the line about my presence—and my request. I took the yellow legal pad I'd stuffed in my purse and doodled. Fifteen minutes later I was still doodling. I went back to Dorothy and repeated my request. She told me it was Sister's day to monitor the playground activities and she would be free in another ten minutes. I went back into my bench-warming, doodling mode.

A nun, garbed in a long black habit with a white wimple covering her hair finally appeared at the far end of the long hall. She seemed to float toward me. I've always thought that nuns must be taught how to move about as if they were on a transporting walkway, like those in airport terminals.

I stood up as she approached. "Good morning, Sister."

In a very low voice, with precise diction, she answered, "Good morning to you Ms. McMuffit. I am Sister Bridgett. How may I help you?"

"Call me Annie, please, Sister. I need to know the name and address of the people who adopted a one-year-old girl from here. Probably around 1928 or '29."

Sister eyed me I thought somewhat suspiciously. "May I know why you are asking?"

"I work for Joe Carter. He lives in Carterville and I've recently discovered a diary that tells of a little girl being brought here for adoption." Then I decided to tell a teensy weensy white lie. "The man I work for hired me to find this woman. She might possibly be the last of his family, except for him, of course."

"I see. Well! Let's go to the record room and start our search. You're the second woman to ask in the past two months so the information shouldn't be too hard to locate."

Hot Ziggity, I only had to tell one fib, and it worked. I didn't even need to hire a lawyer.

I walked and sister floated to the end of the hall where she ushered me through a door identified as "Record

Room." All four walls in the room were lined with shelves full of ledgers.

Sister wafted around as she silently checked dates on several rows of stacked books then pulled two from a bin marked "To storage."

"Here they are, Annie. Good luck with your quest." She guided me to a small table and placed the books in front of me. "I have a meeting to attend in five minutes. When you are finished please leave the books on the table. I'll tell Dorothy. Please check out with her as you leave."

It was exciting to be this close to my goal of finding out about Bernice, Polly's daughter. My trembling fingers turned the heavy yellowed pages of the record book for 1928. Nothing there, so I slid it away from the top of the one dated 1929. I opened it and discovered what I searched for on the page dated January tenth.

Record of Bernice Chloë Carter

Given name at birth... Bernice Chloë Carter

Gender... Female

Birth date... July 15, 1927

Home delivery by...Thadius Miller, M.D.

Child's address...1202 Carter Street, Carterville, Illinois

Placed for adoption... September 2, 1928

Age adopted... One year five months two days

Date adopted... January 10, 1929

Adoptive parents...
Mother... Mary Milner
Father... Chester Milner
Address...612 Oak Street, Canton Illinois

40

AT TWENTY MINUTES TILL NOON I turned the car into the driveway and parked by the apartment in Carterville. The sky had opened up before I began the trip back from East Peoria. It dumped six inches of snow in three hours, covering everything outdoors. I love how it looks when snow sticks and piles up in rounded mounds over house roofs, barns, hedges, and tree limbs. The whole countryside reminded me of a picture on a Christmas card.

Following a snowplow as it worked its magic on Route 24, I had little difficulty driving but it took some concentration. I speculated off and on about what a grown-up and grown-old Bernice might look like. I thought she would probably resemble the portrait of Polly hanging in the parlor over the mantelpiece. Again, I wondered if she were the "Berni" that Polly had scratched in the dirt as she lay dying. I wanted to tell Joe about this new information I'd discovered in East Peoria, and once again needed to show him a diary.

I hadn't told Mrs. B that I'd be gone today, so she expected me for my Wednesday soup and Spam sandwich. I carefully picked my way through the snow to the stairs leading up to the apartment. The snowstorm had slowly turned into an ice storm. I threw my gear inside the door to deal with later. Lunch came first.

The weather was getting worse. A smooth shell of ice covered everything in sight. Branches, heavy with ice, fell from the tall oak trees on the property. It downed electrical wires and caused a power outage in the house. I'd been looking forward to dinner tomorrow at the B's house, but now I wasn't sure if that would be possible.

Fortunately, Mrs. B was able to use the gas stove to fix lunch. I gobbled my food and went upstairs to work on the third floor.

I hoped I wouldn't have to give up going to Canton on the Friday after Thanksgiving. I wanted to chase down additional information on Bernice Carter's adoptive parents. My thinking was that as soon as I found them I might have something solid to tell Joe when I showed him the information about the adoption. It hadn't dawned on me till now that Joe wasn't the only Carter left. I now knew he had a cousin named Bernice.

It was frigid in the house, so I put on a heavy fur coat from one of the armoires and worked a little longer. The cold house and lack of light, however, caused me to quit early.

Slipping and sliding, I made my way to the apartment. There was no electricity there either. So I piled all of the covers I could find in the place on top of the bed and topped them with the fur coat I'd been wearing. I crawled into bed with my clothes on and before long my body heat warmed me.

I awoke at midnight, sweating. The electricity must have come back on. Maybe all was not lost for turkey dinner tomorrow at the B's. I climbed out of bed and headed to the kitchen where I raided the refrigerator. After devouring all the leftover food, I took a shower and crawled back into bed.

In the morning I called Mrs. B to ask if I could bring something over for Thanksgiving dinner.

"Only your lovely self, Annie."

* * *

The turkey was super good, as was the cornbread stuffing. Definitely not Mrs. B's usual culinary offering.

Later, Joe, Mr. B and I told her how good the food had been as we four sat in the living room. She seemed pleased with the praise and smiled. "Thank you."

Joe patted his stomach contentedly and loosened the button on his pants.

Mr. B's stomach was already round. But I'd bet it would be a lot rounder tomorrow. I looked down and checked my own tummy for a bulge. Oh, oh, I'd be dieting tomorrow. I too had made a pig of myself at the table laden with traditional Thanksgiving fare. We three declined Mrs. B's famous blackberry cobbler but told her, "Later, for sure."

We played cards and I asked Joe where Monica was spending the day. He said she went to her folks and had given him the day off. Before I went back to the apartment we all forced ourselves to try the cobbler with heavy cream. Mrs. B loaded me down with leftovers to stock the tiny fridge.

She tucked the recipe for her cobbler into my sack bulging with goodies.

41

IN CANTON THE NEXT DAY, I drove past Willow, Spruce, and Pine, then turned left onto Oak Street. A seedy looking box of a house sat between 610 and 614 with no street number showing. I parked three doors down from it, walked to the house, and opened a sagging, one-hinged wire gate. I could see the outlines where a house number had once been. The only number left hanging was a black metal 6 and it had come loose. It hung upside down and now looked like a 9.

After knocking on the screen door, I couldn't hear sounds inside. I knocked louder, shouting, "Hello, hello, anyone home?"

No answer! Now what to do?

I thought about turning this attempt at detecting into a new predicament for Ms. McMuffit...Investigator. This would be my first stakeout. Shades of Sherlock Holmes. I already had Venus as my Dr. Watson, but she wasn't here. *Think! Think! Think!* Slapping my forehead with the palm of my hand I tried to dislodge any loose ideas in there.

I walked back to the car and scrunched behind the wheel, hoping no one would see me. Surveillance was in progress.

From my view I could see that the small area around the weathered gray house was as unkempt as the yards across from the orphanage. A saggy wire fence encircled the junk-filled yard. The makeshift gate with its one hinge, pretended to stand guard. The larger pieces of junk in the enclosed area must have been accumulating for—God alone knew—how long. It looked like leftover furniture from Goodwill, recycled many times. Tin cans and broken bottles lay scattered everywhere I looked. Dirty plastic bags snagged by the wire fence fluttered in the wind. A garbage can sitting on the front porch spilled its contents.

Ater three hours of surveillance with no activity whatsoever, I needed to find a bathroom—in a hurry—so drove to Main Street to the Burger King. I slammed on the brakes and bailed out of the car, one thing in mind. Wouldn't you know it? A busload of seniors had just emptied out and the lineup for the bathroom was long. Very long.

As I jumped into the middle of the lineup, one old biddy, who looked like a plucked chicken, kept going "tsk, tsk" with her tongue and glaring at me. I wasn't a senior citizen, but I had rights too, and my priority was to whizz without humiliation.

At long last I emerged from the bathroom, with a smile on my face. I decided not to fight the long food line, so left. I zipped around to the drive-through, got two Whoppers, and was back on the road again in five minutes. I wanted a cup of coffee but remembered, what goes in comes out, so I passed up the liquids.

I sped back to Oak Street, parked and devoured both sandwiches. I was really tired of waiting for something to happen. I felt like a frozen Annisicle. Going to the door at 612 I knocked on it again and thought I heard the sound of a TV. I knocked louder when no one answered.

The TV sound went off and a grumpy voice called, "I'm coming, I'm coming, don't knock the damned door off its hinges." Hinges seemed to be a problem around here. The door was jerked open and a small, really old man stood there, framed by the screen door.

"Whatyawant?"

"Sir, I'm Annie McMuffit. I'm trying to locate a Mr. and Mrs. Milner. The last known address I have for them is this one. I think they must have lived here years ago."

"No one here by that name now," he growled, and slammed the door in my face.

I'd been hoping for something simple like they still lived here after seventy years. I sighed. *"Get real, Annie."*

Someone in the neighborhood might remember Mr. and Mrs. Milner. I knocked on several doors of the nearby houses without success. I finally roused a senior woman four doors down from 612 who recalled the family. She said she used to babysit for their daughter, Bernice. She also told me that both parents were dead and she hadn't seen hide nor hair of Bernice since she was a little tyke. I thanked her for the information, disappointed that I hadn't discovered where Bernice could be found. It was dark by then so I drove back to the apartment in Carterville to fret.

Maybe tomorrow would be more productive.

42

A WALK AROUND THE OUTSIDE of Carter house helped clear the cobwebs from my brain. I was ready for lunch by the time I got to the back door. As I reached for the knob it turned slowly, the door inching open. I heard voices murmuring but couldn't hear any words. Making an exit from the kitchen was the woman I suspected was Ron's grandmother.

Oh boy! Now if only her name was Bernice my job of finding the mystery woman would soon be over.

Mrs. B stood directly in back of the woman. When she saw me standing there, she said, "Come back in Lydia, I want you to meet Annie." She waved us in through the open door, before shutting it against the cold.

Dang it, the woman's name is Lydia.

"Lydia, this is Annie McMuffit. Remember my telling you that she is here to do an inventory of the house for Joe. Annie, I want you to meet Lydia Snyder. Lydia is Ron's grandmother. She and I were school chums. We went to grade school together in Canton."

Lydia and I exchanged smiles, shook hands and both said, "Hello," at the same time, along with the insincere words, "Pleased to meet you." I've often wondered about that, when you meet a person, and tell them you're pleased to meet them, how do you know you're pleased to meet them until you get to know them?

Lydia said, "I really must be goin'."

"Be careful. The roads are a slippery mess, Lydia"

"I heard on the TV news the snow'd be comin' hard through the night," Lydia said. "The roads are gonna' be real bad tomorrow, don't ya' know?" She pulled the door open, one hand on the knob as she prepared to leave.

She turned around and said to Mrs. B, "Goodbye Bernice."

In all of the detective novels I'd read over the years, there is always a defining *"AH, HA!"* moment when everything comes together. This was my *"AH, HA!"* moment. I think I've found my Bernice.

After Lydia left I said to Mrs. B, "I've never known your first name was Bernice. Everyone I've ever heard speaking to you, or of you, calls you Mrs. B."

"Well, now you know," she growled and made a vinegary face. She grabbed the frying pan out of the oven, slammed it down on a stove burner, and added Spam.

I sat at the kitchen table watching Mrs. B slam bang the lunch preparations. I thought back to that time at Polly's funeral, when Joe first introduced her to me as Mrs. Bagley. I remembered thinking then that she was built sturdy, more like a man. She was close to six foot tall with skinny long limbs and her feet were turned out in an awkward, splayfooted stride. Now, as I looked closer at her, I could see that her eyes were the same cobalt blue as Polly's in that portrait in the parlor. The eye color was the only part of Mrs. B that looked even remotely like Polly. The rest of her was a female version of Harry Cody. It wasn't any wonder that I'd thought the picture of Harry in the old newspaper article about the Cody gang in Peoria looked like someone I knew.

I needed to go slowly as I trawled through Mrs. B's brain for information. She was banging pots and dishes around. A warning! I'm sure she was telling me by her body language and behavior that she knew what was coming. I started my fact-finding fishing expedition in as non-threatening a way as possible. "Mrs. B, I need to ask you some questions. They'll probably not be easy for you to answer."

Arms folded over her ample front she said, frowning, "Well, how do I know if I want to answer them, till you ask."

I jumped right in that opening with, "I found all of those diaries that Sarah wrote and I've started putting two and two together. You've probably read them all. I know for a fact that you read the one about Sarah murdering Harry Cody. I saw you reading it here in the kitchen. Am I right?"

"Aren't you a miss nosy poker," she hissed, cutting her eyes at me. "What are you getting at?"

"Only that you knew Sarah had murdered Harry Cody and that Polly helped her bury him out in back here. I think you didn't want anyone to find out about that. You probably thought I'd uncover the truth."

Silence. Then, "I couldn't care less if that dirty business came out."

"It was you, who tried to frighten me away, wasn't it Mrs. B?" I asked compassionately.

She ignored me, turned aside.

"I went to East Peoria to St. Mary's orphanage and read the information pertaining to Bernice, Polly's child. Sister Superior said that you had been there two months earlier."

She whirled back to face me. "That woman had no right!" she spat out.

"I know that Polly Carter was your mother, and Harry Cody your father. That must have been quite a shock to you when you finally figured it out.

"Mrs. B, was it you who tried to frighten me away?"

Silence. Then with a quivery chin she answered, "Yes, it was me, Annie. I'm so sorry for all of that but I never did harm you. Just wanted you to leave. I knew you'd turn over the apple cart, and you have."

Flinging her body into the chair opposite mine, she dropped her forehead onto folded arms laid on the table top. Taking one long, loud sigh she wept for a solid twenty minutes as if a rain cloud had ruptured. Her gut-wrenching sobs filled the room.

I left her alone with her misery and started a pot of coffee. I patted her on the back a few times, murmuring, "There, there," with an eye to stopping the waterworks. It only increased the flow of tears. I finally gave up, and let her long overdue cry run its course.

The tears finally stopped. She hadn't moved. With her head still on her arms I heard her whisper to the table, "I did it. I killed Polly."

Mrs. B's fabric of lies had started splitting at the seams. She sat upright. The truth poured out.

"I guess Polly must have been my mother, Sarah my grandmother, and Harry Cody my father. That makes me Joe's cousin. I've been a damned slave my whole life to that mean old woman."

"How did you happen to live next door here?"

"I was adopted by Mary and Chester Milner when I was almost two. They lived in Canton. I learned how to take care of sick people by looking after my adoptive mother from the time I was ten. She died of cancer when I was sixteen. Then I took care of my adoptive father. He had heart failure. He passed when I was eighteen."

"Did you ever look for your birth parents?"

"No! They gave me away like I was a bag of garbage. They didn't want me. And I didn't want them. I never tried to find them but did wonder off and on who they might be.

"I met Willie at a dance in Canton the year father died. We dated awhile. Willie and me, we got married. I answered an ad in the paper about being a caregiver to a middle-aged woman, Polly Carter. The job offered the use of the house next door and we didn't have much money. I had all that experience from taking care of Mom and Pop so the trustees who'd run the ad hired me. We moved in that house and lived there all this time. When I was twenty, Doc Miller told me I could never have children. I was free to keep being a caregiver for Polly. Fifty years I took care of her. Fifty long thankless years never knowing she was my birth mother. To think of all of those wasted years I romanticized about who my real mother and father might be, and why they put me up for adoption."

"Tell me about the night Polly died, Mrs. B."

"I found those diaries four months ago and have been reading them. When I came to the part about the murder, I went crazy with anger. How on earth did they get away with murder for all of those years? When I read the 1928 diary, that part about Polly's baby being named Bernice I got goose bumps. I just knew it had to be me. I went to the orphanage in East Peoria two months ago and found that information about myself. Sarah, my grandmother, murdered my father. Polly, my mother, helped her bury him out back here. The longer I thought about what all happened years ago the madder I got.

Mrs. B continued spewing. "I finally worked up enough courage to come over here that night Polly died. I went to her room and point blank asked her if she remembered helping bury Harry's body after Sarah murdered him? Then I asked if I was her daughter?"

"Oh, my God, how painful for you, Mrs. B. What did she tell you?"

"She got up out of that bed. Just stood there and shook all over. Wouldn't look at me. Wouldn't answer me. Looked at the wall in back of me with her old faded dead eyes. Her devil jaw clamped shut. I was filled up with anger. It boiled over. I pushed up against her. She wobbled over to the stairs that lead to the widow's walk. Tried to get away from me. I was so God-damned mad I actually did see red."

I needed to keep her talking. "What happened then Mrs. B?"

"I wasn't about to be shut out again. I pushed that old woman up those stairs. Said 'You want to go up there? Then let's both go up there, but you're gonna' answer me in one place or another.' I pushed and pulled her up those stairs. When we got to the widow's walk I asked her again. 'Am I your daughter?' She wouldn't say a word. I took her old bony shoulders in my hands and shook her like a dog does a rag. She tried to get away. I gave her a shove. She fell through that rotten wood railing. I didn't know what to do. I needed to borrow some time. I called 911. Made up a story about a murder on the other side of town. I didn't want the police to be over here on this side of town and come here from the station looking for trouble. They sure would have found it."

I asked, "Was that the article about the murder on the other side of town when the helicopters flew over Carterville? The one I asked you about when I first came here?"

"That's the one. I knew you'd be trouble for me. I was right."

"Tell me the rest of the story, Mrs. B, okay?"

"I left Polly lying there on the ground where she landed. Went home. I didn't even care if she was dead. Never one time in all these years did I ever think that Polly Carter might be my mother. I hate her."

"Did you take Polly's diamond necklace?"

"It flew off her scrawny neck. Landed in the dirt. I picked it up and shook the dirt off it and came in here. I lobbed it up in that chandelier. Thought it would blend with the light fixture. It did till you found it. It belongs to me. After all is said and done I'm still her daughter."

A fresh batch of tears ran down Mrs. B's cheeks wetting the bib of her washed-out denim apron. She wiped her eyes, sniffled, and asked, "Now what's gonna happen to me, Annie?"

"I don't know, Mrs. B."

I stepped to the phone, dialed Chief O'Reilly. When he answered I told him, "You need to come to the Carter house, Mrs. B has something to tell you."

EPILOGUE

MY ANTIQUE BUSINESS IS BOOMING these days as a result of the transfusion of money I earned in Carterville and poured into its coffers. July is pushing August now. It doesn't seem possible that almost a year has gone by since Joe Carter first entered Annie's Attic and hired me to appraise his assets after the death of his Aunt Polly.

Sitting at my desk in the antique shop's office, I was having a cheese, cracker, and coffee break while mulling over the events that took place in Carterville. I wanted to sort out what happened there and what became of the people I'd met.

Joe's auction had been held in January of this year as planned. It was a huge monetary success. The buy-to-sell customers and the antique collecting enthusiasts came from miles around. Some of the eager ones arrived the night before and opted to sleep in their cars. They looked well prepared for camping out in winter weather. I'd seen many innovative ways to keep themselves warm.

The cut glass and brass chandelier in the parlor sold for six thousand dollars, two thousand over what I thought it might bring. The child's caned oak rocking chair Bernice sat in when Sarah took her last baby picture went for two hundred and eighty dollars. In the room where I found that cherry wood spinning wheel on the third floor, I'd unearthed two large boxes of ironstone Flow Blue dinnerware by Staffordshire. That lot sold for twenty six thousand dollars. Highly collectible! The name Flow Blue describes the blurred effect of the cobalt, oriental motif decorations. They were gorgeous pieces displayed on a table, under a spotlight. I'd also uncovered, in another of those third-floor rooms, two pieces of furniture by Gustav Stickley, a china cabinet and library table. Stickley's furniture has a Missionary Spanish influence, square with a simple design. Both went for a total of nineteen thousand dollars.

After the auction Joe handed me a check for five thousand dollars. He told me it was a bonus for the outstanding job I'd done for him. He promised a glowing referral to help catch future customers. Joe said I'd gone way beyond what the job called for by finding Polly's diamond necklace, (not appraised yet), the body of Harry Cody, and uncovering Mrs. B's involvement in Polly's death.

Mrs. B is the person who haunts my mind frequently, poor Mrs. B--Bernice. Chief O'Reilly arrested her the day she'd confessed that she pushed Polly, causing her to fall from widow's walk. She was jailed, and summarily let out on bail. Mr. B called me in late January to say that Mrs.

B had suffered a severe heart attack. The emergency room doctor couldn't save her. How sad her life had been.

Poking my nose into a mystery is one of my favorite things to do. I've been looking into how to become a bona fide mini-private eye, nothing involving a gun. I could never shoot another human being. My goal was to gently explore and resolve any customer's problem. I didn't think I'd need a license for that, but you never know.

Joe had his garage sale in March. I didn't go to it in Carterville but heard it was a success. Joe said Ron helped with the sale and was a whiz at selling. I regretted not getting to know Ron better after being put off by my instant aversion to him. As it turned out he was really a true friend to Joe. I thought about why I'd taken such an instant dislike of him and decided it was probably because he reminded me of my sneaky ex-brother-in-law Tony. After my divorce, and to this day, I make believe Tony doesn't live anywhere on the face of the earth. It works for me.

Last month, Mr. B phoned Venus and asked for a date. She told him that she'd think about it but at the present time she was dating Oscar, the man who works part time here in Annie's Attic. When Oscar heard about Mr. B calling Venus he walked around for a week with such a sulky, pouting lip that I thought he might trip on it. Go figure! Here was Venus with two men interested in her and I'm still on the shelf. Maybe I should ask her how she does it. Nah! It would probably cramp my style.

Maybe that was it? Maybe I don't have a definite style when it comes to attracting a mate. I might have to work on that.

Jake, the bartender at the Duck Inn in Foggy Bottom, where I first met with Joe, hadn't troubled me since that one time at the Sleep Inn motel. I heard later that he'd been convicted for raping a woman in Canton. He's doing hard time in Joliet prison. I felt remorseful that I hadn't turned him in when he tried to assault me at the Sleep Inn. Maybe if I'd told the police then, I might have saved the woman he raped.

My nosy next-door neighbor, Myrtle, still lives in the same house and is still snoopy.

Joe tells me that Sparky, his three-legged dog, developed a love interest with Monica's white poodle, after he and Monica married. He said the two dogs are with each other most of the time. Propinquity has done in many a male, be it man or dog. Joe said Sparky follows Josephine, Monica's dog, everywhere she goes and in-between they snuggle together in her red doggie bed.

Sugar, my cat, is her same wonderful white fluffy, furry self. She still patrols the shop and brings me a stray mouse now and again as a present. She has developed an entourage among the customers. Many of them come in at least once a week just to visit her. She does love to be stroked, verbally and physically. Sometimes I think she understands the English language, maybe it has something to do with the tone of a voice that tells her how absolutely magnificent she is. Sugar thinks she is royalty.

What started my reminiscing about Carterville was the birth announcement that arrived in the mail this morning. Joe had enclosed a news-filled letter. Their baby weighed in at a bruising ten pounds two ounces, a boy, they named Joe Carter, Jr. Joe had never been a father. His excitement and pride over the birth spilled out on the paper as he wrote. He said he bought the baby some presents, a baseball bat and glove, and a pair of miniature boxing gloves. The baby celebrates his birthday on the same day our nation celebrates Independence day. Born on the fourth of July, Joe calls him his little firecracker.

Joe and Monica decided not to sell that big old Carter place. They moved into the emptied out house after their wedding and began renovations. I had shuddered when I first thought about Joe beginning a family at his age. He was old enough to be Monica's grandfather but it all seemed to be working out for them.

Not the end of the Carter line yet but I honestly think their gene pool could stand some chlorine.

I heard a loud crash coming from the shop and went to investigate. It was Venus. She had entered the shop with an elderly gentleman in tow and slammed the door shut.

When Venus saw me she breathlessly said, "Annie, come over here and meet Mr. Shaw. Wait till you hear what happened to him. He told me that when he got home from church yesterday he discovered his apartment had been turned upside down. Someone stole everything from his secret room. He says he can't go to the police."

Hmmmm! My gray matter kicked in. I extended my hand as I said, "Nice to meet you, Mr. Shaw. Here. Let me give you one of my cards."

ANNIE MCMUFFIT

CONFIDENTIAL INVESTIGATIONS

CALL 309-DETECTS